SAIL AWAY TO LOVE

Lady Catherine is at the château of the Marquis de Clichy in 1789 when the French Revolution starts. She escapes with the Marquis's son, Bernard, her companion, a crippled maid and a young couple with their baby. They disguise themselves as a bargee family and sail down the Loire to Nantes. Bernard thinks Catherine is frivolous until he is injured, then he admires her bravery when she arranges their passage to England.

ANNE HOLMAN

SAIL AWAY TO LOVE

Complete and Unabridged

LINFORD
Leicester

First published in Great Britain in 1996
under the title
'Escape to Love'

First Linford Edition
published 1998

British Library CIP Data

Holman, Anne
    Sail away to love.—Large print ed.—
Linford romance library
    1. Love stories
    2. Large type books
    I. Title
    823.9′14 [F]

ISBN 0–7089–5228–3

Published by
F. A. Thorpe (Publishing) Ltd.
Anstey, Leicestershire

Set by Words & Graphics Ltd.
Anstey, Leicestershire
Printed and bound in Great Britain by
T. J. International Ltd., Padstow, Cornwall

This book is printed on acid-free paper

1

"LET me pass — you bullies!" Young Lady Catherine Fray, mounted side-saddle and dressed in a stylish riding habit and feathered jockey cap, hoped she looked and sounded more confident than she felt.

She'd been enjoying her summer-morning ride — until her way was blocked by these two surly peasant women.

When they started throwing stones, Catherine began to feel scared. But her dark eyes sparkled determinedly.

"If you don't let me open this gate, I'll . . . I'll . . . "

But what could she do — except turn back? But why should she? As an English guest of the Marquis de Clichy she was entitled to ride where she pleased on his Loire chateau estate.

Then remembering the rumours of

peasant unrest in France, she realised it had been foolhardy of her to gallop ahead of her groom.

Her mount gave a piercing whinny as a stone hit him. Taken by surprise, she felt herself slip as the beast shied. The next moment, Catherine's body was jarred as she hit the ground and her startled pony bolted.

"Oh, no!" she muttered, getting to her feet.

Now she would have to defend herself as best she could only this time it was two against one! Catherine watched as the two French women began to close in on their prey. And, standing her ground, Catherine formed her small hands into tight fists as she had seen her brothers do.

Beads of sweat formed on her brow. Her ankle-length riding habit didn't give her the freedom to run — or even to move with the ease her foe had in their shorter skirts and aprons. She shivered with apprehension, sensing the evil-faced peasants were out for blood.

Suddenly the advancing pair froze. A scream from one of them made Catherine look in the direction she was pointing, to where a horseman was galloping towards them.

"You little imbecile!" the rider's deep voice shouted as he drew nearer. "You should not have outridden your groom, Lady Catherine. Those women are brigands — troublemakers — they could have killed you!"

She flushed with embarrassment seeing it was the Marquis's handsome eldest son who had come to rescue her, and her dimpled smile vanished at being called an idiot — although she knew she deserved it.

She secretly admired Bernard, but he treated her like a brainless schoolgirl who'd just left her classroom. He seemed to admire the French ladies who were far more sophisticated in their dress and behaviour.

He rode his horse close beside her, and, lowering his arm to encircle her slight body, drew her up on the saddle in front of him. Thrilled to be riding with the best horseman in the district her hands clung to him.

Bernard was tall, good-looking and as proud as his father, the Marquis de Clichy. But the Marquis was far more charming towards her than his son.

Turning to gaze up at Bernard's stern, dark eyes, straight nose and firmly set lips, she said, "My lord, you do not have to be quite so impolite about my, er, mistake — I was not aware that the revolutionists had spread as far as the Loire Valley, and if you knew, you should have informed me."

"I had no wish to frighten you, Lady Catherine."

"I'm not scared of peasants!"

"Your companion, Madame Barbier, is terrified," he said, smiling at her untruth. "She's heard the mob in Paris has taken the Bastille fortress. She wants you both to return to England immediately."

"But Madame Barbier promised me a visit to Paris."

"That is most unfortunate for you, my lady. However, some of us have more to lose than a mere shopping expedition."

She flushed, realising he had succeeded in making her seem like a spoiled and irresponsible schoolgirl.

Catherine knew the dear old Marquis had given his son complete charge of the estate during his enforced stay at court in Versailles and that included being responsible for his relative and companion, Madame Barbier, as well as herself who had come to France to finish her education.

Arguing with Bernard to prolong her stay would be futile; she knew she would have to return home. Catherine's exasperated sigh made him give a short laugh. He wheeled his horse around then urged the animal to canter.

"Forward, my beautiful Golden Star," he commanded softly.

Furious he always seemed to find her at fault, she said, "My lord, I do believe you prefer horses to women."

"Horses are highly-intelligent creatures, Lady Catherine. Females frequently behave as if they have little sense."

Flabbergasted by his insult, she was not able to think of a suitable retort, especially as she knew she'd invited his sarcasm.

They rode through wild-flowered meadows, passing the estate woodlands, until the great Château de Clichy came into view. When they arrived at the stables she said, "Thank you for your assistance, my lord."

Dismounting, Bernard gave her his ruggedly attractive smile. He lifted her down from his horse in the extensive stable yard constructed to take the Marquis's heavy gilt coach and team of horses.

"Your company is always a pleasure, Lady Catherine. You are the prettiest young lady I've ever met." His ebony eyes twinkled down at the expression of surprise on her vivacious face. Then taking her small hand he bowed to kiss it in the gallant French fashion.

Her cheeks became rosy with the flattery of being complimented like an elegant French lady — until he added, "May I remind you not to be so hoydenish in future?"

Gritting her teeth, Catherine forced a smile. If she wanted to impress him as being a mature woman, she would have to hide her dislike of his teasing.

She replied sweetly, "And may I remind you, my lord, that English girls are bred to show spirit — we are not merely frivolous dolls!"

A broad smile appeared on his lips as he bowed to acknowledge her barb. He then threw the reins over his horse's head and Catherine heard the clip-clop of hooves as he turned away and led the animal into the stables. Bernard always preferred to rub down his own horse rather than allow a stable-boy to tend his favourite Golden Star.

★ ★ ★

Madame Barbier was in a state of agitation. Her hands fanned the air as she waddled towards Catherine.

"We must leave France instantly, ma chérie!" Her contralto voice and double chins trembled as she enveloped Catherine to her ample bosom. "I've heard there are riots everywhere — we must flee this very minute!"

Catherine was used to Madame Barbier's hysterics. She had a great fondness for the plump widow, who had been more than just a governess to her after her mama had died, and was now her devoted companion.

"Calm down, Madame Barbier," Catherine said cheerfully as she extracted herself from the embrace. "I know we must return to England, but we must pack our things first." Catherine thought keeping her companion busy might prevent her from panicking.

When Madame Barbier was engrossed sorting their clothes with the help of a maid, Catherine said, "I'll go and change for dinner, then I'll find Bernard to ask if he will arrange a coach for us early tomorrow morning."

She kissed her companion on both cheeks, whispering, "Courage, Madame, we will soon be back at my father's house in Somerset."

Somewhat pacified, Madame Barbier said, "Do wear your rose silk gown this evening, ma chérie. It is a great shame you cannot stay in France long enough to wear it at a ball. You look so charming in it with your ebony hair decked with flowers and ribbons."

Catherine smiled, deciding she would please Madame Barbier and wear it — wishing also to see Bernard's reaction when she was all dressed up.

Having changed, with a French maid to ensure she looked her best, Catherine flitted down the château's wide staircase, through the grand reception rooms where the elegantly-dressed family and guests were listening to music, conversing, or playing cards. They did not seem in the slightest bit worried about the stories of peasant riots.

Not seeing Bernard, she asked a footman where he was and was directed towards the stables.

When she found him, Bernard was holding a paper and appeared ill-at-ease. He didn't seem to notice she was wearing her best gown as his troubled eyes sought hers.

"What's the matter, my lord?" she enquired coming close to him.

Bernard put his finger to his lips and looked around before he put his arm around Catherine's shoulders and pushed her gently into an empty horsebox. She began to protest loudly.

"Shush!" he whispered. "A messenger has just come from Versailles with this letter from my father. He fears we might all be in danger. It has been reported that many Loire châteaux are being attacked by mobs."

Catherine's hands went to her mouth to suppress a cry.

"My father tells me we must be wary

of everyone — even our servants."

Catherine shuddered. She looked up at Bernard's noble face and felt thankful she could trust him. Just then footsteps could be heard. Bernard lifted his head to listen as he motioned to Catherine to be silent.

A coarse voice could be heard hissing, "Wait, we must take a quick look around the stables. That sharp son of the Marquis is often around here with the horses — he's the one we'll have to watch."

Catherine instinctively moved nearer Bernard as they both crouched down, listening to the men tramp up and down the stalls.

"No, he ain't about. Now as I was saying, the old Marquis is at Versailles and will be trapped by the citizens of Paris."

Their guffaws sent shivers down Catherine's back.

"So we'll set his pile o' bricks alight tonight, eh?"

As the men drifted away Catherine

saw a look of horror on Bernard's face.

"So, we have little time," he said grimly.

Catherine made to run for the château, but he caught her wrist.

"You must stay here while I go and warn everyone. I will send Madame Barbier to you, then you must both go to the coachman's cottage. Our coachman, Jacques, is a good man. Tell him from me he is to arrange for you and your companion to start immediately on your journey to the coast."

"Surely I can do something to help you."

He shook his head as he gave her a sad smile.

"No, there is nothing you can do, Lady Catherine." He looked deeply into the dark wells of her worried eyes. "Except . . . look to your safety."

With a tender look in his eyes, he said to her, "Promise me you'll stay here until Madame Barbier joins you."

Catherine nodded, feeling unwilling to see him go, yet knowing it would help him by not having to worry about her if she agreed to stay.

He hesitated, then embraced her swiftly with a gentle kiss on her lips which sent shivers of excitement through her. Giving her a final fleeting smile he walked quickly out of the stables.

Catherine ran after him, but stopped by the stable door. Clutching the door frame to steady herself, she watched Bernard's broad-shouldered figure go out of sight — and wondered if she would ever see him again.

★ ★ ★

Waiting is so hard, Catherine thought as she paced up and down the stables. She longed for Madame Barbier to appear.

Although waiting is not as hard as learning that your family is in danger and your home is going to be destroyed,

13

she chided herself. She knew Bernard's mind must be in turmoil with little time to warn his family, friends and staff, before the arsonists attacked.

Sorrowfully she went to Golden Star's stall to stroke and talk softly to him but a noise outside made her freeze. Raucous cries signalled an approaching mob. Catherine darted into the horse's stall and cowered in the straw.

"Pity the Marquis isn't at the château," a rasping, high-pitched woman's voice rang out. "I'd enjoy stringing up that high and mighty aristocrat!"

Sickness attacked Catherine as her body quivered. What had the Marquis done to deserve such hatred? She shivered again.

"Citizens!" a voice bellowed. "Our time has come. Light your torches and follow me. We will bring the cleansing fire to this aristocratic vermin nest . . . "

His voice was lost amidst the roar of the crowd's approval.

14

Keeping hidden, Catherine peeped through a crack in the wooden planks. Malicious enjoyment could be seen on the vandals' faces as they armed themselves with pitchforks of hay, and lit torches ready to set off on their destructive rampage.

Catherine was worried that Madame Barbier still hadn't come. The mob had left the stables — but might return to find her.

She decided to take Golden Star to Jacques' cottage. Having no strength to saddle the big horse, she unhooked Golden Star's bridle from where it was hanging in his stall. Grooms usually bridled her pony for her, and she found it difficult to put the bit in the animal's mouth.

Golden Star was too high for her to get up on, so she had to take him outside to the mounting block. Warily she looked out over the stable yard. There was no-one about.

Leading the horse, she stopped him by the mounting block, skipped up the

15

steps and eased herself on to Golden Star's back. It was difficult in her long dress to sit astride but she knew she had to try.

She decided to ride a short distance towards the château, just a little way along by the ornamental gardens just in case Madame Barbier and her maid might be coming to find her.

It was evening by now and the moonlight cast a sheen over the pattern of shrubs and clipped hedges.

"Madame Barbier!" she called out delightedly seeing two shadowy figures making their way towards her carrying what looked like travel bags.

"Oh, my God!" Catherine gasped as the moon came from behind a cloud and showed the two figures clearly. They were not her companion and maid, but the two peasant women who had attacked her earlier.

"Look at that rider's gown. Citizen, we've found ourselves an aristocrat!"

"It's that silk-stocking that slipped our net this morning — catch her!"

Catherine's heart thudded as she struggled with the immobility of panic. Then her commonsense told her to move. She knew if those spiteful females got hold of her this time she would have no chance.

If it were not for the peasants' greed — they were carrying arms full of spoils from the château they were reluctant to drop — they might have sprung and dragged Catherine from her mount.

Thankful she was riding a well-schooled horse, Catherine turned Golden Star around, and hearing angry yowls and curses behind her, she urged Golden Star into a gallop.

Riding away from the château, on towards the forest, she didn't stop until she had taken the horse under cover of the trees. Then she looked back to see orange and black smoke in the sky.

The Marquis de Clichy's château was on fire and flames were licking up into the sky. Catherine felt her mouth dry. She prayed everyone had got away safely. She was safe herself . . . only she

17

was lost, alone at night, and dressed in an evening gown. Somehow she had to find Jacques' cottage.

It was cold with no cloak to cover her, and eerie to be surrounded by shadowy trees. Every crackling twig, scampering of rodents' feet, and hooting of an owl, made her start. She gritted her teeth, and told herself she would soon be out of the woods. Allowing Golden Star to have his head, she set off along a footpath.

2

"**H**OLA! Hola!" A man was calling after her. Lost and thoroughly chilled, after riding through the moonlit forest for what seemed like hours, Catherine was delighted to meet a party of horsemen.

But as they cantered up and surrounded her she feared she was unlucky.

"The woman's an aristocrat," one of the riders spat. "Look at that fancy gown she's got on."

"She's riding a good bit of horseflesh."

"And she's not so bad herself."

Leering faces in the semi-darkness made Catherine recoil. Struggling to overcome her fear, she sat straight on Golden Star's back trying not to show it. Praying she had the courage to die nobly if these brigands were going to kill her, she wondered fleetingly if her dear Madame Barbier had suffered that fate. And Bernard, too.

"Wait . . . I think I recognise this woman . . . yes, she was staying at the château. She may know where that sly son of the Marquis is hiding out."

So Bernard had not been caught!

"Take her to Citizen Picot — he'll know what to do with the baggage."

Catherine breathed easier. They were not going to harm her — yet. A bullish man leaned forward and grabbed the reins from Catherine's hands, and flinging the leather straps over Golden Star's head, he led Catherine's horse forward.

As the mounted party pounded along, Catherine, riding with no saddle and afraid of falling off, clung to Golden Star's mane.

"Stop! Please go slower," she begged.

But her cries were either not heard, or were ignored.

She was becoming almost too exhausted to remain on the horse's back by the time they approached a small town. The riders clattered down the cobblestone street, and eventually halted outside a high-storeyed, timber house. Lights were coming from the casement windows.

Feeling battered, Catherine slithered to the ground. Rough hands dragged her to her feet and her limp body was hauled into the house. In a candle-lit room, she was dumped on the wooden floorboards.

"Citizen Picot, we found this woman in the forest. She escaped when we set fire to the chateau."

A chair was scraped back and she heard footsteps. Buckled shoes appeared near her. Catherine blinked as she looked up. An elderly gentleman, with parchment-like skin tight over his bones, was staring down.

"Citizens, this is no way to treat a young lady."

Monsieur Picot's cultured voice sent a flutter of hope through Catherine as she rose unsteadily to her feet. Perhaps he would help her. Feeling her head spinning, Catherine put her hand to her forehead.

"You are a little fatigued, my dear?"

"Yes. I do feel a big giddy."

Monsieur Picot snapped at one of the men.

"Get the kitchen wench to bring the young lady a drink."

The order given, Monsieur Picot turned back to Catherine.

"I detect a slight foreign accent in your voice, mademoiselle."

"I'm English, monsieur."

"Ah. Your name?"

"My father is the Earl of Shendish."

Immediately she regretted her words. Was she wise to tell him that?

His thin lips twitched as he walked to his desk and sat down regarding her. His finger scratched under his wig while he pondered. The door opened and a wretched little girl was shoved into the room carrying a glass of wine.

The poor child looked as though she had just been woken up and was rubbing her eyes. Her scrawny body was covered with a ragged dress, and her feet were dirty. Catherine also noticed she was afflicted with a club foot.

Her heart went out to the unfortunate child seeing she showed signs of maltreatment, too. Some bruises were not hidden by her rags.

"Ah, Violette. Give the drink to the young lady."

Violette's enormous brown eyes surveyed Catherine, making Catherine wonder if the pathetic-looking little creature was quite as young and helpless as she appeared to be.

"Violette," Monsieur Picot said, "this young lady will be staying here. You are to take her to the visitors' room and look after her."

"Yes, Citizen Picot," the girl said dutifully, as one bony hand moved a strand of her lank hair from her face and tucked it behind her ear.

Monsieur Picot then addressed the guards.

"Let it be known that no-one is to

touch the young lady. Is that clear?"

Catherine was thankful to hear these instructions as the rough guards scared her. She finished her wine, and wished she had eaten something that evening because she began to feel light-headed. So when Violette lit a candle and beckoned her, Catherine did not feel like arguing. Where else could she go that night anyway with no money or warm clothing?

As they climbed up the steep flights of stairs to the top of the house, Catherine was as fearful as a prisoner being led to a prison cell.

The cold attic room had one small window. There was a rush-seated chair, and the wooden bed had a straw-filled mattress and a hairy blanket that looked as though it would scratch her skin.

Although she would have loved to wash, she considered how hard it would be for the lame maid to haul a pitcher of hot water up the long flight of steps in darkness.

"Don't bother to bring me any water tonight, Violette. I've already disturbed your sleep. Go back to your bed."

"Thank-you, mademoiselle," she chirped before hobbling out.

Feeling too exhausted to stay awake and bemoan her fate, Catherine slept. But before she did, her thoughts turned to Bernard's ruggedly attractive smile. Had he escaped and abandoned her? And what had happened to Madame Barbier?

* * *

In the morning, Violette woke her as she hobbled in and filled the bedchamber washbasin with hot water.

"You slept well, mademoiselle?"

Surprisingly Catherine had, although her barren surroundings immediately reminded her of her captivity.

"Violette, I must see Monsieur Picot. I want to return to my home in England. And I can't do that without some travelling clothes and money."

"You will have to see one of the National Guards. I daren't ask."

Several hours went by and Catherine's optimism sank. Her constant requests to see Monsieur Picot were ignored, and when she tried to find his room she was rudely brushed aside by burly guards.

"Go away, he's busy," she was told.

"You'll have to wait until Monsieur Picot wants to see you," Violette explained with the submission of a servant.

Catherine was cross — unused to being treated with such dismissiveness — but realised she would have to accept a captive's lot, and just be grateful her circumstances were not worse than they were.

She noticed the guards were using Golden Star as one of their horses. She was so glad Bernard didn't know about it.

Bored having nothing to do all day, and afraid of remaining by herself as the guards taunted her, Catherine wandered down to the kitchen. Seeing little Violette being overworked, and cuffed by the cook, she offered to learn a few simple cooking tasks so that she could help the crippled maid.

"But your hands will get red and sore like mine," Violette cried.

Catherine was aware that her best silk gown would get ruined, too, but she replied cheerfully, "Don't you worry, Violette, just pass me that apron, and show me what to do."

Violette was amazed to see a lady doing domestic work and giggled.

"It's as well the cook daren't beat you, mademoiselle!" She chuckled.

Catherine was surprised at her clumsy efforts to master simple domestic tasks peasant girls learned as soon as they could walk.

"No, do it like this," Violette would say, showing her.

As the days went by, Catherine felt pleased as she gradually became more skilled, and she found chatting to Violette passed the time as well.

Violette questioned Catherine about her rich life in England and how she came to be in France — and in her present predicament. Inevitably, Catherine mentioned the man who was constantly on her mind; the man who had given her her first real kiss on the lips.

"Tell me about Bernard," Violette said, as they sat out in the sunshine shelling peas.

"He's tall, and very good-looking," Catherine said, stopping her work and gazing up at the sky remembering his dark, handsome features.

"How old?"

"Much older than me. I'd say about twenty-eight. I suppose that's why he seems so much more mature and confident."

"Is Bernard the Marquis's heir?" Violette wanted to know.

"Yes, he is."

"Then the revolutionary guards will want to catch him."

"I fear so." Catherine sighed.

Being a prisoner at the region's National Guard Headquarters, Catherine heard snatches of the men's talk and learned some harsh facts. France was bankrupt; many people were unemployed. Two bad harvests in a row had resulted in high prices — some peasants couldn't afford bread, their staple diet. No wonder there was a revolution brewing! The peasants were blaming the French king, and hated the uncaring aristocrats.

"You like Bernard, don't you?" Violette asked with a knowing grin.

"Yes, I do — though I have no idea why. He's forever criticising me."

They had finished shelling the peas and Violette said, "If Bernard notices you — even to find fault with you — then he cares about you. No-one cares about me. There's only the cook and he'll be after me if we don't get back in the kitchen soon and start on the other vegetables."

When they were in the kitchen Catherine said, "I think Bernard has forgotten about me."

"Don't say that. He probably doesn't know where you are."

"And we can't send a message to him, Violette — because we don't know where he is, either." Catherine couldn't stop the tears from falling.

"Don't cry, mademoiselle," Violette said kindly. "From what you've told me, Bernard's not the kind of man to run off and leave you to your fate."

"You are right, Violette. Besides, I shouldn't grumble — not when I've seen everything you've been through in your life."

Violette, who was now peeling potatoes, told Catherine her story.

"My papa was a tenant farmer until his pigs got swine fever, then the greedy seigneur demanded more tax than my father could give him. So we were turned out of our farm cottage. We walked for miles and miles with our cart looking for work. It was a bitterly cold winter. First my baby brother, then Mama became weaker . . . "

Violette stopped talking and wiped a tear from her cheek. Remorse smote Catherine. She'd never fully understood before how hard life could be for some.

"We didn't have enough to eat, mademoiselle . . . when little Henri and Mama died . . . poor Papa lost the will to live, he just became thinner and thinner and faded away . . . "

Catherine looked sympathetically at the disabled girl who had suffered so much. Violette went over to put the chunks of potato in the big black pot hanging over the kitchen fire.

"So I came here, mademoiselle — at least I get something to eat everyday, and it's warm in the kitchen in winter."

★ ★ ★

Early the following morning, when the girls were busy plucking chickens, Catherine was confronted by one of the guards.

"Come with me. Citizen Picot wants to see you."

Catching a glimpse of the pain crossing Violette's pinched face, Catherine's heart plunged. Was she to be sent home at last? Were the two friends to be parted?

"Violette, I . . ."

But the maid had grabbed a bucket and hobbled out towards the yard well, obviously unwilling to say goodbye. Catherine felt her throat tighten.

She was marched along and pushed unceremoniously into Monsieur Picot's study. Monsieur Picot sat at his desk, looking just as she'd seen him three weeks ago. But Catherine's eyes were drawn to the back of a tall man, dressed in plain ratteen breeches, with the bright tricolour cockade of the revolutionaries in his hat.

"So this is the English aristocrat you hold for ransom. I am prepared to sell her back to her father for three thousand livres, Citizen Picot."

The man turned and Catherine

was sure. She would recognise that handsome face anywhere. Yes, it was Bernard!

The voice she knew — but his disguise baffled her. Why was he behaving as if he did not know her? Had he become a revolutionary?

As soon as she opened her mouth to question, Bernard stepped smartly up to her and smothered her mouth with his hand.

"Hold your tongue or I shall be forced to slap you!" he rasped in her ear.

Shaking with dismay, her face reddened as she pressed her lips together. That the Marquis de Clichy's son should behave in this disgraceful way shocked her deeply.

"Here is the ransom money, Citizen Picot. Leave it to me to get what I can from her father."

While Monsieur Picot's eyes gleamed at the huge amount of money he was presented with, Bernard said, "I'll take the chit now."

Before Catherine could gather her wits, Bernard had grasped her firmly around her legs and had hoisted her over his broad shoulder. Catherine screamed as he carried her out of the room.

"You have a fine set of lungs on you!" Bernard remarked jovially.

The spectacle of the English aristocrat being borne off like a squealing piglet brought every man who heard the commotion out to see the fun. Much to Catherine's chagrin, Bernard even seemed to be enjoying himself!

Yet he quickly entered the stables and found the horse he had arrived on. He lifted Catherine on to its back, while he leaped on his own horse, Golden Star. Gathering the reins of Catherine's horse as well as his own he rode out towards the courtyard gate, waving to the watching men who seemed to be slightly in awe of this mysterious stranger.

From her position behind Bernard, Catherine suddenly became aware of a child darting out towards Bernard. The girl came dangerously near the horse's hooves, and Catherine held her breath, watching Bernard using all his skill to avoid Golden Star from trampling on the pleading child.

"Bernard! Bernard. Take me with you!"

Violette was crying out to him as she lifted her small arms — Bernard seemed unsure of what to do next. For a moment Catherine's mind spun. She felt certain now that Bernard had been using a ploy to rescue her, and if they were delayed, they might be captured. But in her heart she felt she could not abandon little Violette.

"Bernard," she shrieked, "please take Violette!"

In an instant Bernard had obeyed her request. He swooped to scoop up Violette, and placing her behind him with the instruction to hold on tight, he was ready to leave again. The men's roars of laughter had ceased.

"What's he picking up the kitchen

brat for?" a voice hollered.

"I think he's tricked us, citizens. Stop them!"

"Bolt the gate!"

As several guards ran towards the courtyard gates, one leaped to grab Golden Star's reins but Bernard struck him with his whip. Catherine watched quivering, but with a determination to make a run for it.

Bernard was as quick as Golden Star was well-schooled. Neatly they wove past the guards while Catherine urged her horse close behind until they were through the gateway and out into the street.

"Here, take your reins, Lady Catherine. Ride as fast as you can," Bernard yelled. "Keep up with me."

Fired with the thought of freedom and the dire consequences of being caught, Catherine rode for her life, as shots sounded in her ears. Bernard needed all his expertise to gallop riding with Violette, but they had a start on the guards who were scrambling to the stables to mount and follow them.

Leaving the town behind, Bernard headed for the cover of the nearby woodland. Catherine, breathless, but exhilarated with the hard riding, relaxed as they slowed the horses amongst the trees in a sunlit glade.

"Thank God we are safe!" she exclaimed, and laughed with relief as they dismounted for a rest.

"We are not away yet!" Bernard rebuked her as he lifted Violette to the ground. His mild rebuff reminded Catherine that he still regarded her as an irresponsible chit, and she bristled — until she reminded herself that Bernard had risked his life to rescue her.

"Thank you for coming for me," she said gratefully.

For a while his full attention was on her — concern for her apparent on his face — and she felt a surge of happiness. Putting her arms around him she lay her head on his chest, hearing the beating of his heart. As she felt his hands come protectively around her she wished she could remain in his arms for ever.

"Did they hurt you, Lady Catherine?"

"No, my lord, I am well."

He stroked her hair tenderly and chuckled.

"You are courageous, my little one. I'm sorry you had to suffer as a prisoner for so long."

Easing her to arms' length his eyes looked deeply into hers as he said, "It was not until I spotted a guard riding Golden Star that I discovered where you were. Please forgive me for your undignified release — it was the only way I could think to get you out."

"I'm sorry to have cost you so much."

"Sometimes we have to pay dearly for the things we want."

Catherine felt herself blushing but she could not help grinning at him.

"Madame Barbier, is she well?"

Bernard suddenly turned his head, listening. Hearing nothing of their pursuers he said, "I don't think they have our scent. Yes, Lady Catherine, Madame Barbier is safe. She is waiting for you at Jacques' cottage. I will take you there shortly. First we must shake off the guards hunting us. Wait here while I reconnoitre — I won't be long."

As he disappeared amongst the trees, Catherine became aware of Violette and felt a stab of guilt as she rushed up to the neglected girl.

"Oh, Violette, I'm so glad we managed to take you with us."

"I've always dreamed of getting away — and now I have." Violette's wistful face broke into a cheeky smile.

"Quickly . . . remount." Bernard came crashing back through the undergrowth. "The guards are searching this area. I'll take you back to the château to hide, whilst I lead the guards on a wild goose chase."

3

THE blackened ruins of the great château shocked Catherine. Bernard rode around the desolate building until they reached the kitchens.

"There are wine cellars below the kitchens where you can hide," he said, leaping off Golden Star then helping the girls dismount.

Flinging himself back on to Golden Star's saddle he took the reins of Catherine's horse.

"I'll lead your horse for awhile to make a false trail, then release him," he said looking anxiously behind. "I hope to God we've not been followed."

"Take care, Bernard," Catherine said, her voice full of concern.

"Make sure you two keep out of sight until I return," he ordered. "The guards may come looking around here." Golden Star snorted, pranced around, and then at Bernard's command, raced off. Sick at heart to see him go, Catherine said a prayer that no harm would come to him.

"I suppose we had better go and hide," she said, not liking the idea of hiding in a dark cellar. "Come on." She gently pushed the maid forward while Violette gazed up in awe at the biggest building she had ever seen.

Inside they were met by a scene of devastation. Broken glass and crockery littered the flagstones of the kitchens. Everything useful had been stolen, the butteries and pantries ransacked.

"I think these steps lead down to the cellars." Catherine shuddered, reluctant to go down into the wintercold underground rooms.

"It's a pity we can't find a candle anywhere, Violette. Hold on to my hand and step where I step," she said, pretending she possessed more courage than she felt — and hoping there were no rats about.

She was thankful for Violette's chirpy conversation during the long hours they huddled in the dank place behind some wine barrels.

"Bernard is so handsome!" Violette exclaimed. "And yet he has a deeper quality as well. His eyes speak of secrets — warm and exciting. I'm sure he is the man for you, mademoiselle."

"I admit I am attracted to him," she confessed, "but he treats me like some foolish girl."

"Oh, no, mademoiselle, he is merely anxious no harm should come to you. I think he will realise one day he loves you."

"Now you're just being silly, Violette!"

"No, I'm not. My grandmother was a clairvoyant — I, too, have her sight, mademoiselle."

"Don't keep calling me, mademoiselle. I'm a Lady," Catherine snapped, annoyed with Violette for continually pointing out facts to do with the marquis's son.

Later, Violette said, "I can't stop

my teeth from chattering." She was hugging herself to try and keep warm.

"Neither can I," Catherine said, and felt around for some sacking to cover them. But there was no comfort to be found in the cellars. "We'll die of cold if we stay here much longer, Violette. We must go up and get into the warm sunshine. I'm sure the revolutionary guards haven't come to the château — they're far away chasing Bernard by now."

They blinked in the bright sunlight as they crept warily outside.

"I can feel myself thawing out already!" Catherine exclaimed throwing back her head and stretching out her arms towards the hot sun, and feeling the comforting heat melting her frozen body.

"Shush! I thought I heard a cry," Violette said.

Both girls immediately hid themselves behind some kitchen herb shrubs. But although they listened for some time they heard nothing.

"It's getting late — I'm hungry," Catherine said.

"You wait here, mademoiselle . . . I mean, m'lady . . . and I'll creep back into the kitchen and see if I can find anything for us to eat."

After a while Violette returned empty-handed.

"There's nothing. Every crumb from every pantry has been cleaned out. No apples in the barrels, no cheeses. Everything's gone."

In the kitchen gardens they were luckier and found some ripe peaches. Hiding behind the beehives they sat eating while watching all the time in case Bernard should return.

"Listen! I'm sure I heard another cry," Violette said.

Catherine licked the delicious juice from her lips and said, "There are lots of wild animals around — that's probably what it was."

Later, the unmistakable sound of a horse approaching startled them, until they found the courage to peer out to see who it was.

"It's Bernard!" Violette shrieked.

Catherine's eyes closed in a thanksgiving prayer, then she rose and ran to greet him. The hounding both he and his sweating horse had endured made Catherine's heart go out to the exhausted pair.

"So you're both all right then?" he asked, gasping for breath as he wiped the perspiration from his drawn face.

As Catherine assured him they were well, she put out her hand to sweep back a lock of his dark hair that had fallen over his eyes. He had scratches where bushes had ripped his skin. He had lost his hat, and his clothes were absolutely filthy, but there was nothing Catherine could do for him.

He was more concerned about the welfare of his horse, until Violette piped up, "We heard a cry once or twice, my lord, but we've not seen anyone."

Bernard looked anxiously towards the chateau.

"I'd better go and take a look. Here, Lady Catherine, take Golden Star and walk him slowly over there into the orchard, out of sight."

The long shadows of the summer evening made patterns over the neglected château kitchen gardens and orchards. Catherine was pleased to hear Bernard calling them after a few minutes.

Rushing to meet him she was amazed to see he was not alone.

A young, fashionably dressed couple were with him.

"May I introduce my cousin, the Duc de Verry, and his wife, Madame la Duchesse, and their baby son, Charles."

Catherine suppressed a giggle at their stiff, courtly bow and curtsy, which under the circumstances, seemed comical. For the young pair were obviously destitute, their costly clothing as soiled and torn as her ball gown.

The fragile-looking Duchesse held a tiny, wailing baby in her arms.

"So this is who I heard crying,"

Violette exclaimed delightedly. "Let me hold him, madame. I love babies."

The Duchesse, Catherine felt sure, would not have dreamed of giving her son to such a shabby-looking girl under normal circumstances, but she seemed only too glad to have someone to hold the child for a while.

As Violette started rocking and clucking at the snuffling infant, the Duc explained, "Several weeks ago our Château was attacked, and knowing my uncle, the Marquis de Clichy, to be a kindly man, we came here hoping he would take us in . . . but we saw here, too, the mob had struck. We stayed here because we had nowhere else to go. We were hungry and searched the kitchens — but we have now eaten all there was left."

Catherine felt compassion for the helpless, young family, and was delighted to hear Bernard say, "You must come with us to Jacques' cottage. Violette and the baby will ride Golden

Star — the rest of you will have to walk I'm afraid."

The Duc darted back to fetch their few belongings, and the odd party set off towards the coachman's cottage.

Aware that Bernard was tired out and had now been saddled with three more lives to protect, Catherine was not surprised to see him scowling. He must be tempted to take off on his own. Seeing how well he'd played the part of a revolutionary, she knew he could easily pass himself off as a gentleman of no consequence and ride alone to safety in Spain or Austria.

Getting to the cottage seemed to take for ever. Everyone was tired and hungry, and the Duc and Duchesse's elegant but impractical clothing and heeled shoes made it difficult for them to walk the woodland paths.

It was dark by the time they arrived. The lights shone from within the cottage and Jacques' dog came rushing out to greet Bernard.

"Oh, goodness, Catherine!" Madame

Barbier exclaimed with glistening tears of joy running down her plump cheeks. "I'm so thankful to see you safe — but look at the state of you! Your lovely gown . . . it's in tatters!"

Catherine fell into her companion's arms sobbing with happiness to see her safe.

"Now, ma chérie, I must get you clean, and into some fresh clothes."

Madame Barbier seemed totally unaware of the others until Catherine said, "Madame Barbier, we must get the baby washed and fed first."

"Baby? What baby?"

"The baby son of the Duc and Duchesse de Verry."

When Madame Barbier's eyes looked around and spotted the young couple she clapped her hands together joyfully.

"You don't mean to tell me that this young man is Hubert de Verry — the talented musician who is now married — and has a son?"

The smiling Duc stepped forward and Madame Barbier squeaked with pleasure to be embraced by a member of her family she had not seen since he was a child.

"This is Gabrielle, my wife. And Violette is holding our son."

"Violette?" Madame Barbier exclaimed sharply, her eyes widening as she took in all these surprises.

"Violette was the kitchen maid at the Revolutionary Headquarters where I was being held," Catherine explained. "She escaped with me."

Madame Barbier glanced sympathetically at the crippled girl holding the whimpering baby.

"Come along in, Violette. We must make that poor baby more comfortable at once." She swept over and, placing her plump hands on Violette's shoulders, guided her into the cottage.

The small cottage was bulging at the seams with so many people, but Jacques and his wife were most hospitable. The baby was soon fed, washed and swaddled in clean linen for the night. Jacques' kindly wife found the old rocking cradle that had served her family's children and Charles was rocked to sleep.

Luckily, everyone seemed to regard the group as friends, and they supped on a tasty venison pottage from a large black-iron kettle hanging over the fire.

It wasn't long before Catherine noticed Violette's head drooping with exhaustion and quickly removed the bowl from her hands before she spilled the contents. Madame Barbier fussed around making sure everyone had a blanket and some sort of pillow for their heads. Soon the silence of the night replaced the day's unusual activities.

But Catherine found it difficult to sleep. Her eyes swept over the sleeping bodies and then she spied Bernard. He'd wrapped himself in his travelling cloak, and was propped up in a corner near the door as if on sentry duty.

As she looked over at him and studied his serious expression in the dim light, she knew he must be more tired than any of them. Yet the pain of losing his home, and the worry of all the people he was now responsible for getting to safety, must be keeping him awake. She wanted to help him — if only he would regard her as a mature woman instead of a capricious chit.

* * *

The morning was well advanced when Catherine awoke to the quiet chatter of everyone in the cottage and the delicious smell of newly-baked bread. Around her everyone was stirring, but when she looked across the room to where Bernard had been sitting, the place was empty.

"Oh, I feel so much happier now!" she heard Violette exclaim.

Catherine smiled, understanding Violette's elation at being free from the drudgery at the Revolutionaries' headquarters. But she — although glad to be released, too — was concerned about Bernard. And with the difficulties they all faced.

"Why, Catherine, you are awake at last." Madame Barbier came bustling up to her. "You must come and wash. I'll get a fresh gown for you from the travelling bag."

Tubbed down, hair soaped and rinsed until it shimmered like spun silk, Catherine felt her imprisonment was finally behind her. Wearing her pretty, flower-sprigged cotton dress and white leather slippers, she stepped outside to dry her hair in the sun.

It was peaceful away from the crowded cottage, comforting walking on the springy emerald grass by the woodlands, and watching some red deer grazing.

"Lady Catherine! Do you have any idea what you are doing?"

Bernard's angry voice cut into her pleasant reverie, and she swung around to face him. He seemed taller and more over-bearing as he loomed over her.

"Heavens, woman, have you no sense? Do you want someone to

see you dressed in your finery? Go inside!"

His withering glare took all the pleasure of the morning away.

"I'm sorry, my lord . . . I did not think, I was just — "

"That seems to be your trouble — you never do think!"

Catherine's cheeks burned. Why did he have to show such anger at her thoughtlessness? No harm had been done. She turned on him defiantly.

"Your manners leave much to be desired, sir! Your father would be ashamed of you!"

To her surprise, he put his hand over his face and turned away, walking towards the cottage as though she had slapped him. Catherine stood watching him until she heard Jacques call her softly.

"Lady Catherine."

Holding a bundle of firewood he'd been collecting he came close to her, "Please forgive the intrusion of an old servant. I couldn't help overhearing what you said . . . "

"Jacques, I regret to say I lost my temper."

The coachman's gnarled hand rested on her arm and indicated she should sit on a nearby log.

"Lady Catherine, I've known Bernard since he was a boy. He's a fine young man. But he is not himself today. He has suffered many sorrows recently. You may not have heard that his father the Marquis de Clichy has been imprisoned in Paris — "

"Oh, no!" she gasped, devastated to hear the news.

"I should also point out, Lady Catherine," Jacques continued, "that the Marquis's son had to shoot Golden Star this morning."

"He killed his beautiful Golden Star?" Catherine couldn't believe it. "But, Jacques, Golden Star was his favourite horse. He adored him."

Jacques rubbed a tear from his eye.

"Indeed, Lady Catherine, it is a grievous blow for him. He told me

55

it was impossible for him to take his horse with him. If he left Golden Star with me it might place me and my family in trouble. Nor did he want to sell Golden Star with the other horses to make some retirement money for the château servants, in case he was mistreated."

Catherine felt stinging tears roll down her hot cheeks and she felt Jacques' hand on her shoulder.

"Go to the cottage now my dear. He is telling the others about your plans to escape."

* * *

"Our main concern is to leave France without being caught — and this will not be easy," Bernard was saying.

His eyes followed Catherine as she slipped quietly into the room.

"To travel across country to reach the ports of la Manche, St Malo or Dieppe, would mean exposing ourselves to the possibility of being caught in the many road blocks the revolutionaries are setting up. The northern ports are well guarded I've heard, therefore, I propose we go west. Take a barge down the Loire — ''

A unified gasp from his listeners made Bernard stop.

"A boat!"

The idea excited everyone's imagination. Loud chatter broke out until Bernard's voice cut it off.

"I have little hope of any of us reaching England!" he bellowed. His fierce eyes made all tongues silent.

"Your imbecilic enthusiasm for a boating expedition on the river overlooks the fact that the vessel will be unpleasantly overcrowded. You will be obliged to dress, and appear by your actions and voices, to be a poor bargee family. I assure you, you will find the trip uncomfortable, tedious, and food will be hard to obtain for so many of us. And you will be in danger every minute."

He had succeeded in frightening the

lot of them but he still continued,
watching them carefully.

"Most important, each one of you
could, by some careless act, betray
us all!"

His belligerent glare rested upon
Catherine.

4

"**I** KNOW you loathe needlework, Catherine," Madame Barbier said. "Take a rest and let me get on with your garment for a while."

Catherine pressed her palm to her aching head.

"Oh, Madame Barbier, I wish I wasn't so thumb-fingered when there's so much sewing to be done."

They were busy making peasant clothes to disguise themselves as a bargee family. While Violette was looking after the baby, and helping Jacques' wife prepare a meal, the women were stitching and the men carving wooden sabots — except for Bernard, who still had not returned from making arrangements about hiring a sailing craft to take them to Nantes.

The air was fresh and sweet outside the cottage, and Catherine breathed in deeply as she closed her tired eyes. I must take care to hide myself, she thought, least anyone passing by the cottage should see me. Finding a secluded spot, she sat down and rested her throbbing head against the bole of a tree — and drifted into a doze.

"What are doing out here? I thought I told you to stay indoors!" Bernard thundered over her. Catherine struggled back to her senses — and her feet.

"I . . . I must have dropped off . . . "

"Don't bother to make excuses, Lady Catherine. I suppose you consider it to be beneath you, to sew like the others."

"No," Catherine blurted out. "My head ached . . . Madame Barbier suggested I . . . " Words failed her, horrified that he thought she had skipped off leaving the others to do all the work.

"Then you must think that we're leaving next week, instead of tomorrow morning."

Her eyes widened and her cherry

lips formed an, "Oh!" Looking with concern at his severe expression, she said, "Is it going to be so soon?"

Immediately his eyes softened. But a moment later his dark brows knit as he said bluntly, "There is no point trying to look innocent, Lady Catherine. I know you to be a thoughtless chit. Just try to remember this. If you land yourself into trouble, you may harm the others — "

"I'm not irresponsible!" Catherine flared, feeling the heat on her face. "One day, my lord, you shall eat your words!"

"That I can hardly wait to see."

Stung by his sarcasm, she turned her enflamed face from him, pressing her lips together tightly to prevent herself from telling him what she thought of his uncivil manners and unfair accusation.

"I'll go back and finish my sewing," she muttered.

"Before you go . . . "

She stopped in her tracks, but did not turn around and allow him to see

61

the tears in her eyes. In grim silence she waited.

"The next time I find you disobeying my orders, madam," he shouted at her, "I'll teach you a lesson you'll not forget!"

How dare he insult her so? She couldn't think for a minute what she'd done to deserve such harsh treatment. As Catherine fled towards the cottage, her anger gradually subsided as she remembered Jacques telling her of Bernard's sufferings and his unselfishness.

Despite her tearful face, she knew she had to join the others — she dare not do otherwise. Hurriedly she wiped the dampness from her face and took a deep breath before entering the cottage.

She could tell as she took up her sewing again, that Bernard had not burdened the party with his sorrows. He knew that it would not help their morale to know that the Marquis de Clichy was imprisoned. Bernard's personal grief of having lost his home and most of his possessions, including Golden Star, he was keeping to himself.

Therefore, the least she could do was to bear the brunt of his ill-humour, keep cheerful and not allow him to rile her.

The others, seemingly unaware of any unhappiness, were bubbling with excitement. Their costumes were almost finished, their plans laid. They were ready to begin their long journey to safety in England.

A crowing cock woke them at sunrise. Catherine always found it hard to get up in the morning, and four o'clock seemed far too early for her. She felt numb, until the scratchiness of the rough material of her peasant dress made her only too aware of the dangerous adventure ahead.

"Take our travel bags out to the cart, if you please, Catherine," Madame Barbier requested, "whilst I'll see if I can help the Duc collect his family's belongings."

Outside it was barely light. Two Percheron carthorses were tossing their heads as though objecting to being harnessed so early.

She saw a powerfully-built peasant wearing baggy pantaloons, a blue smock and a red scarf knotted around his neck, busy loading the cart.

"Give them to me, Catherine."

"Why, my lord, I didn't recognise you!"

"Bernard, please try to call me Bernard. We must not use our titles. Will you tell the others?"

She nodded, knowing she would do anything she could to help him out.

"And ask everyone to hurry, Catherine, as the boatman will be waiting for us."

She was pleased to note the ill-humour of yesterday had vanished. Perhaps he'd had some remorse about the way he spoke to her, and had decided to treat her more as an equal. She gave him a dimpled smile.

As she turned to go he called, "Wait!"

He leaped from the cart and his wooden clogs struck the ground as he walked up to her. She almost giggled seeing his blackened teeth, the stubble on his unshaven face — until he blazed, "Cover your hair!"

She stepped back smoothing her hand over her dark tresses. Her hair was not dressed; all she'd done that morning was to brush it hurriedly.

"Don't pretend to be surprised, Catherine. I know you are aware you're attractive . . . but to flaunt your attributes on this journey would be fatal."

"You are mistaken, sir. I may be young and giddy in your eyes, but I do not flaunt myself as you so crudely put it!"

Her outburst had the effect of silencing Bernard — for a few moments. Then his mouth flickered at the corners.

"I apologise, Catherine. It is not with any intention of offending you that I must ask you to loosen your girdle, and cover your head. You may not realise it, but beautiful hair like yours will attract all kinds of unwanted attention and advances."

Amazed she had succeeded in bringing him to heel — if only for a moment — Catherine said, "Very well, Bernard, I will endeavour to find a head cover. Perhaps Jacques' wife had something I can wear."

She did not like the idea of having to wear a mob-cap all day long, as well as a prickly dress and wooden shoes, but if this was the cost of her freedom then she would have to comply. It wasn't Bernard's fault and she couldn't see him enjoying dressing up like a peasant — he was usually meticulous about his clothes and grooming.

Laughter filled the air as she entered the cottage.

"What frights we all look!" Gabrielle exclaimed, who was normally attired as an elegant French duchesse.

"I think our costumes are splendid." The young duc was strutting around the room in his wooden clogs — until one slipped from his foot and he landed in a heap.

Catherine was enjoying the fun, admiring everyone's attire, until suddenly she recollected her duty and clapped her hands.

"Quickly everyone, Bernard . . . " She flushed, embarrassed not to be giving him a title. "He is waiting for us. Bernard says we are to use our Christian names only and to remember to act as peasants." She breathed more easily. Now she had used his name twice, it would be easier in the future. "Please take a careful look around and make sure you have not forgotten anything."

A sober mood descended as they obediently scrambled for their things, and Catherine found a piece of cloth that served well as a headscarf.

When they were ready to leave, Jacques and his wife were thanked profusely. Genuine tears poured down the old couples' faces as they bid their respected young lord farewell. It struck Catherine how much loyalty, nay love, Bernard seemed to get from everyone.

If only he would recognise my worth and deep regard for him, she thought wistfully.

Catherine made a solemn resolution to keep their danger in mind and to help Bernard in every way, to keep cheerful and try never to complain. Also, having the sense to realise the coming journey could lead them into disaster, she vowed she would endeavour to be brave come what may.

A Loire boatman, wearing the same garb as Bernard, was waiting for the party as the loaded cart swayed towards the riverbank. He was a pipe smoker, and chatted to Bernard in a friendly fashion between puffs, showing as much concern for his unusual freight as his placid disposition allowed.

The shallow river sailing craft, called a chaland, had a single mast with square rigging, main and topsail. It was designed to carry cargoes of timber, sacks of grain or barrels of wine — to be replaced with a load of salt on the upstream journey.

The men stacked the luggage in the hold, leaving only the small cabin space normally used by a bargee family. There was barely enough room for the party to squash in when it rained — although fortunately the weather promised to be warm and sunny and they could camp on a riverbank overnight.

As a farm lad came to collect the horses and cart, Catherine noticed Madame Barbier's eyes fill with tears, and her lips quivering.

"My stomach feels most peculiar, Catherine," she mumbled. "It's terrible to think we're leaving this beautiful Loire valley for ever — never to see its beauty again."

Catherine took the plump lady's hand and stroked it.

"I do understand how dreadful you must feel," she said sympathetically, looking sadly at Madame Barbier. "Just think, we will be sailing along the Loire for days. You will see it in all its glory and will be able to fill your mind with treasured memories you can keep for ever in your heart."

"You are right. Thank you, Catherine," Bernard's deep voice answered.

She looked up, not realising he was so near. Her eyes fixed on his as she regarded him, not able to find the words she so desperately wanted to ease the torment of his heartache. She hoped her empathy showed as their eyes remained locked . . . she wished she was alone with him, so she could put her arms around him and comfort him — but there was no privacy on this boat.

As the sun rose high above the fields bordering the glistening river, Catherine's body felt movement as the boat glided away from its mooring and water slapped against its bow.

There was a hush on board; a strange feeling of suppressed excitement that they had set sail. A nightingale perched high on a poplar tree saw them off with its plaintive melody. Violette announced it was an omen of good fortune.

* * *

Life on board, Catherine considered, was much like a leisurely holiday. As they sailed farther from their pursuers there was a feeling of safety. And they were, contrary to Bernard's prediction, enjoying their summertime sail.

The warm sun on the sloping vineyards not only fattened the grapes; it gave everyone a healthy colour. Distant farm houses and small waterside villages exuded tranquillity. As they were careful to act as a bargee family, they were accepted by the other boatmen passing their chaland.

"I don't find river-boat life too bad," Catherine commented happily. She'd kicked off her sabots preferring to run about barefoot — and would love to be able to throw off her head scarf, too.

"Absolutely not!" Madame Barbier

retorted, whose plump form was restricted.

"I'm sorry you feel uncomfortable," Catherine said guiltily, realising the younger members of the party, being smaller and more lissome, had an easier time of it. She put her arm around her companion, and kissed her cheek saying, "You've been wonderful, Madame Barbier, helping us all when we moor at night — assisting with all the camping chores — I'd quite forgotten how tiresome it must be for an older lady like yourself."

"Don't you worry about me, Catherine. I will manage. It's Bernard I feel for. I'm sure he's worried — he's got the burden of worry for us all."

"Indeed, I've noticed," Catherine said knowing more than Madame Barbier about Bernard's worries. How silent and withdrawn he'd been as they sailed farther and farther away from his homeland. What future had the poor man — as an impoverished émigré?

"I long to help him, Madame

Barbier. I think of him suffering all the time, only when I try to talk of lighter matters I get a curt dismissal."

"Oh, la, la, ma chérie! You cannot expect a French nobleman to be driven to do anything — he must be enticed."

"I don't think he will confide in me," she said shrugging. "He thinks I'm a child — and a tomboy."

"Alors! Show him, ma chérie, that you are an earl's daughter. It shouldn't be difficult for a pretty, young girl like you to make him change his mind about anything."

"But, Madame Barbier, Bernard is so . . . disapproving."

"Catherine, you have a charming smile — use it!"

Bernard was being taught to sail the boat by Joseph, and was learning quickly to manipulate the long baton which was used to steer the chaland. Catherine decided a good approach would be to ask him — when he was not busy — how he was getting on

73

learning to master the mariner's art.

After supper that evening she found Bernard by the river reclining on a grassy bank, away from the chatter and laughter of Violette playing with the baby, while his fond parents and Madame Barbier watched.

He clearly meant to rise and bow when he saw her coming, but seemed to remember he had to play the part of a boatman and remained where he was. Catherine remembered to smile and felt a rising excitement as she commanded his attention.

Lazily watching her sink gracefully on to the grass he thought what a pity it was she had to cover her magnificent hair. How compliant she had been about wearing that awful scarf all day. His eyes scanned her peasant dress thinking how well it hid her neat figure. Spontaneously he smiled at her, deciding if they got out of France safely she should make someone a desirable wife. Yes, Catherine was proving to be a most agreeable girl.

"Ah, Catherine. Have you come to join me?"

"May I?" she asked, sitting down before he had a chance to answer. "Bernard, are you and Joseph going to row us to England?"

"Good Lord, no!" he said with a short laugh. "When we get to Nantes we will have to find a sea-going vessel."

She made the effort to continue smiling as she raised her eyes to look into his — seeing to her surprise that his eyes had yellow flecks that danced quite beautifully in the late evening sun, and his lashes framed them like brown velvet drapes.

She felt slightly piqued to see the amusement on his face by her close observation of him. Becoming rosy she asked, "Then why does it interest you to learn to sail?"

"This narrow river," he said waving his hand towards the river, "will soon be joined by others and will form a fiercely flowing waterway to the sea. Joseph will need help when we get into the surging tidal waters. I'm told they can be treacherous."

Catherine began to imagine the dangers they might run into.

"Do not worry, little one," he breathed, shifting his body nearer her to take her hand and kiss her fingers gallantly.

His touch delighted her and she longed for him to kiss her lips, too, but it was not to be. He got to his feet and, having helped her up, said, "We must get everyone to bed. Joseph plans an early start tomorrow."

5

"HAPPY Birthday, Catherine!" she heard everyone chorus as she arrived for her evening meal the next day. She thought no-one but Madame Barbier would remember her eighteenth birthday — besides, how could they celebrate it?

Seeing their excited faces she was thrilled to find they had planned a surprise party for her. The pleasantly warm summer evening, and the secluded rural backwater where they were camping, made a perfect setting to abandon their peasant rôles and be themselves.

Catherine's delighted smile made everyone happy as she was given her presents.

"Madame Barbier, you are too generous!" she exclaimed as she embraced her companion. She'd been given a single strand of lustrous pearls that Madame Barbier had purchased some time ago, and had kept hidden ready for Catherine's birthday.

"Is it safe for me to wear my necklace?" she asked Bernard wistfully.

He pressed his lips together, raised an eyebrow in mock consideration, then nodded and took the pearls from her hands. Motioning her to turn around, he slipped the necklace around her slender neck and fastened it. Turning her to face him he then removed her head scarf, untying the knot with deft fingers and surprising gentleness.

"There," he said as he stood back to survey her, making her knees feel weak with his heart-melting smile — her eyes glistening as much as her jewels. "You are a beautiful, grown-up lady now, Catherine," he said solemnly. "We wish you all the happiness you deserve." He kissed her on both cheeks, and then on her lips sending her heart fluttering and bringing a bright flush to her cheeks.

The Duc and Duchesse de Very presented her with a delicately painted, circular trinket box of luminous porcelain. Catherine loved it. Such a small box could be safely tucked away in her travel bag.

So, too, could the small, wooden model of a Loire sailboat — a miniature chaland that Joseph had made for her. Catherine admired his skill and told him she would always treasure it.

"I'm sorry I haven't anything to give you, m'lady," Violette whispered apologetically in Catherine's ear. "But I've picked some fruit for our picnic," she said, pointing to a bowl of tiny, wild strawberries.

Touched by Violette's thoughtfulness, Catherine embraced the maid, making Violette starry-eyed. Bernard had a gift for the party, too. He strode to the river bank and hauled out two bottles of white wine that had been cooling in the water.

Catherine thanked him warmly, knowing by the careful way he handled the bottles that this wine would have come from the Château de Clichy's cellars, and would be an excellent vintage.

When everyone had enjoyed their out-of-door feasting on pheasant roasted on the camp-fire, followed by some fresh crusty bread and cream cheeses Joseph had bought from a nearby village, Catherine was amazed to learn the best of the evening was yet to come.

Delving into his luggage, Hubert, the young Duc, found his treasured violin. He removed it carefully from its case and began to tune the instrument.

The sweet, joyful sounds, when he started to play, filled the countryside and took Catherine's breath away. His playing was magical.

"Hubert, you're a genius!" she exclaimed, clasping her hands together.

"Yes, indeed he executes his pieces with great feeling," Madame Barbier smiled as she tapped her foot rhythmically in time to the melody.

"Come on, mademoiselle, dance for

us!" Joseph called, as he sat contentedly puffing his pipe.

Catherine's face fell. The gavotte Hubert was playing could not be danced without a partner. But before she had time to decline, Bernard stood before her, and with a courtly bow, offered her his arm saying, "Allow me, madame."

At first hesitant and a little shy with him firmly holding her hand, she felt stiff and awkward, as though her feet didn't want to respond to the music.

Bernard's deep-toned voice prompted her, "Place your right foot so . . . "

The warmth of his fingers touching hers, the rapture of the music, more intoxicating than the supper wine, inspired her to dance.

As she remembered the steps, her body moved in time to the music. As if bewitched, she found herself floating in harmony with her partner.

The sensation of dancing with this man, his closeness, sent ripples of pleasure through her. She instinctively smiled as she danced and fluttered her eyelashes at his bemused face.

Holding her a trifle more firmly, she thrilled at this intimacy, knowing Bernard was responding to her coquetry.

Unaware of their audience, their eyes met and held. Struck by his show of tender passion Catherine felt a pang of love for him so deep and powerful she knew she would cherish him in her heart for ever.

"You dance well," he breathed.

"Not at all badly for a hoyden, my lord?" She grinned mischievously.

He gave a chortle making her giggle with pure joy. The tune changed to a minuet, and with easy grace they performed the slower dance movements still gazing steadily at each other.

When the dancing was over, there was another surprise in store as Bernard had rigged up a swing over a sturdy oak tree branch. Some rope from the boat and a piece of spare planking which served as the seat made it look inviting.

"I don't think I've ever seen a swing before," Violette said ecstatically.

Gabrielle sat with her baby on the swing first and moved gently to and fro, while the baby clapped his chubby hands and laughed as he enjoyed the rhythmic motion. The Duchesse sang in a sweet voice an old French nursery song which had choruses everyone joined in.

Then it was Violette's turn on the swing.

"No!" she cried. "It'll make me sick!"

But Bernard ignored her squawks, and lifted the small maid to place her firmly on the seat. Then he gave her a gentle push.

"Let me off!" Violette hollered, but as she got used to the motion and began to enjoy the experience she was, to everyone's amusement, laughing and complaining at the same time.

"Now, Catherine," Bernard's teasing eyes turned to her. "It's your turn."

Catherine's laughter turned to shrieks

of fright as Bernard pushed the swing higher and higher . . . but her heart was singing like a love-bird as she flew in the sky.

★ ★ ★

That night Catherine lay under the stars and thought that it had been the best birthday she'd ever had. There were so many memories of the evening she would never forget.

And she was in love with Bernard. It was both tremendously exciting, and at the same time painful — because how did she know if Bernard had any deep feelings for her?

One thing was certain, however, there couldn't be a worse time to fall in love. They were caught in the middle of enormous trouble — and heaven knows how it will end, she thought, turning restlessly and feeling too wide awake to sleep.

After a while, she became aware of someone coming, and remembering her hair was loose and might attract attention, she melted into the dark shadows of nearby bushes. But her eyes opened wide, because the tall figure walking purposefully away from their camp was Bernard.

Curious to know where he was going, she followed as he headed for a farmyard, and watching him as he began stooping every now and again as though picking something. She was fascinated. She considered disturbing him but he'd disappeared into the barn. A minute later he'd reappeared carrying a sack of something heavy. Perhaps it was something like potatoes, for what else would there be on a farm?

So, she thought, that's what he's been doing, collecting vegetables for us — and picking up some eggs, too.

But why was he doing it at dead of night? Then the awful truth struck her! He was stealing food!

Blood rushed through her head causing it to throb. She could hardly believe Bernard would do such a thing.

The country peasants were poor; they had the greatest difficulty paying their high taxes to the church, and could not afford to lose any of their natural resources, Violette had told her.

Her opinion of Bernard plummeted and she leaned against a nearby tree trunk, devastated to think the man she loved was behaving like a criminal.

She thought back to the meals she had enjoyed. They had set off with some food, but a simple calculation told her that with so many mouths to feed those provisions would not have lasted the long journey.

They ate fish, of course — Hubert had become a good fisherman. But the chickens, venison and vegetables that had appeared for the cooking pot — Catherine had never questioned where they had come from.

True, Joseph occasionally stopped by a village, and bought some bread but to think now it was becoming apparent most of their food had been stolen! Bernard was no better than a river pirate! With her head lowered in disappointment, she was returning to her bed when firm hands gripped her.

"What are you doing wandering around at night?" Bernard sounded more puzzled than annoyed.

The fright she got made her stiffen, but finding who it was holding her, Catherine relaxed and clung to him.

"I . . . couldn't sleep, Bernard," she said in a timid whisper, wishing she had the courage to confront him with her discovery and tell him she'd found out he was a thief.

His hands were caressing her long, silky hair giving her comfort, allowing the knowledge that he had been stealing food to be forgotten. As he hugged her closer she instinctively pressed herself to him, putting her fingers on the nape of his neck, and stroking the dark curls of his peasant hairstyle.

"You're beautiful, Catherine," he murmured as his mouth travelled up her creamy neck and found her lips. Lost in the bliss of his embrace it came as a shock when he suddenly withdrew his lips.

"You must get back to bed," he said, yet seeming unwilling to release the soft body in his arms. "It's not safe for you to be wandering around at night. There's danger — "

"I know, my love." Catherine sighed heavily. "But I am willing to risk — "

"No, Catherine," Bernard said, shaking his head. "Nothing is worth risking your own safety for. No matter how you may feel at the time. Please, Catherine, you must return to your bed."

Dizzy with the pleasure she had enjoyed, yet bewildered by the sensual feelings he had aroused, Catherine turned and ran towards her bed beside Madame Barbier's large, snoring form.

★ ★ ★

In the morning, Catherine asked Madame Barbier confidentially, "Have we some money with us?"

"Certainly we have."

"I mean, are you giving money to Bernard for the food we are eating?"

Madame Barbier looked astonished.

"Whatever has put that idea into your head, ma cherie? Of course Bernard has never asked me for any money!"

Catherine knew she could not pursue the subject without telling her companion what she'd discovered. So she told herself that although she found the pilfering Bernard was doing was regrettable, it was something she couldn't do anything about — even if she ate as little as possible, the others needed food.

Deeply troubled to have responded so readily to Bernard's embrace, and at the same time knowing him to be dishonourable, she baffled him by her cool behaviour towards him the next day.

He noticed her toss her head and walk away when he gave her a smile. She seemed to want to avoid him, and he felt strangely hurt, wondering if she was the kind of girl who enjoyed flirting with men. He would have liked to have the opportunity to talk to her and find out why their seemingly close relationship had suddenly fallen apart.

However, other things grabbed their attention.

"The river current is becoming faster," Hubert commented as the chaland zipped along.

"And it's much wider now," Violette shrilled.

They all realised they had now passed the quieter reaches of the great river and were now heading toward the busier, wider waterway, where the smaller sea-going vessels could make their way up the Loire.

Joseph could see his passengers were becoming anxious and called to them, "My friends, do not have fragile hearts. I, Joseph, have sailed this boat to Nantes for many years."

Everyone was grateful to hear Joseph's reassuring declaration and turned their attention to the altered scene. The tranquil hamlets they'd passed earlier were now replaced by larger fishing villages, and towns whose rooftops filled the horizon.

There was plenty to see: waterfront houses; splashing watermills; fishermen, and womenfolk scrubbing their washing. Shouting children played on the sandy banks, wading up to their knees in the little waves coming towards the river's edge.

They were sailing close to a river tow-path where horses were used to pull craft upstream when the wind was absent, when they heard Bernard yell, "My God!"

Catherine's head jerked around to see what was the matter.

"What is it, Bernard?"

"Look! A troop of National Guardsmen is riding along the tow path! Warn everyone."

Fear gripped her stomach as Catherine scrambled to tell the others.

Trapped on the boat near the path — as another chaland was passing them on the far side — there was no means of hiding from the column of riders bearing down on them.

Were they still being hunted?

"Keep occupied. Remember you are a bargee family," Bernard hissed.

Just as the riders thundered alongside, and seemed to be riding by, baby Charles, sensing the tense atmosphere, began to bawl. Several guardsmen turned to look in their direction. Catherine held her breath as she shut her eyes praying they would not be recognised.

"You woke our baby, you noisy devils!" Joseph shouted. "Get off with you!"

Catherine's heart pounded as one tough-looking guard broke ranks and wheeled his horse to confront the boatman.

"Hold your tongue, you oaf, or I'll fish you out of the water for my breakfast!"

A hushed gasp came from the party. Joseph laughed boldly. The guardsman sent a torrent of abuse at the boatman, then spurred his horse to a gallop to regain his place with the receding troop.

"Do not concern yourselves." Joseph looked at them cheerfully. "There's always banter between the landsmen and us sailors — they expect us to insult them."

Shaken after the danger had passed, the party were unable to regain their carefree spirits. Somehow they knew they were sailing into troubled waters . . .

"Those guardsmen are heading for Nantes," Bernard said grimly. "I regret to tell you we will be seeing many more. Nantes, Joseph tells me, is a hotbed of the citizen's militia. We also have to pass a total of thirty toll-gate check points before we reach the port."

A sigh of dismay ran through the boat.

"Indeed, we have come to the most hazardous part of our journey," Bernard informed them. "In the next few days, when we are in Nantes, you must all take the greatest care. Do exactly as you are told, and leave me to organise everything."

His arrogance nettled Catherine, but she had to admit he was the only person capable of arranging their escape to England. Later she had to admire his cool confidence as she saw him bribe officials to allow the fugitives to pass each toll-gate without being searched. She also could not help being impressed by his newly-acquired skill at sailing.

"Take care for the tourbillons!" Joseph yelled as they used the fixed oar as well as the baton, to steer clear of the dangerous miniature whirlpools which formed by the bridges. Ominous sucking noises could be heard coming from the whirling water.

Gabrielle cuddled her baby to her breast. Madame Barbier clutched the side of the boat to steady herself and Violette lost her normal cheeky smile. Catherine tried to lighten their despondency by telling them a white lie that she was confident that all would be well.

But when she got the chance, she questioned Bernard. He'd been so occupied with sailing he seemed to have forgotten her less friendly manner.

"Do we have to go to Nantes? I have a strange feeling about that place."

She was near him, trying not to look him straight in the eyes — but could not resist doing so. She blushed furiously thinking how much she would like him to put his arms around her and kiss her.

"Yes, we must, Catherine. At the port of Nantes we have to leave this river craft and it's the best place for us to find a passage on a ship to take us to England."

Chilled by his words she gave a quick shudder, and his hand moved to cover hers protectively.

"Don't fret, Catherine," he said looking steadily at her troubled face, and thinking that anxiety may be the

95

cause of her coolness towards him. "I have a plan."

Before she could question him further, his attention was taken by a two masted, square-rigged bugalet, which appeared to be coming uncomfortably close to their comparatively small craft.

Soon there were luggers in profusion about the wide river and Bernard was helping Joseph to sail by these great sea-going vessels.

"By Gad! I say, look over there everyone — there's an English schooner!" Hubert shouted dancing up and down with boyish enthusiasm.

Catherine thought for a moment that Bernard was going to hit him with his baton. Instead he fumed, "Hubert! How many times do I have to repeat: you're supposed to be a peasant? Talk like one, you idiot!"

His wrath made the party fearful. They already felt jittery sailing into the busy port of Nantes.

Tall rigged ships, as well as smaller craft, surrounded them. They heard the piercing cries of the sailors and the constant shrieks of the seagulls swooping around them. Sawing and hammering came from the shipping yards as they sailed by.

There were so many riverside taverns, warehouses, workshops and chandlers — it was all so different from the gentle Loire valley countryside they had become accustomed to.

Catherine, like the others, was agog watching the activities and feeling as insecure to be in this bustling maritime environment. Only Joseph and Bernard seemed confident.

"Just look at them poor slaves!" Violette said with feeling, pointing to a chained gang of dejected black people being driven along the quay.

"This town has grown rich on that loathsome trade," Joseph remarked with disgust. "Us Loire boatmen will have no part of such cruelty."

Nantes, Catherine decided, was an evil place. She hoped their stay there would be short.

6

IT was unnerving when Joseph made for a deserted quay and secured his chaland fast to a boat ring under a massive quay wall.

"Are we going to leave the boat here?" Madame Barbier's trembling voice sounded in Catherine's ear.

"Apparently we are," Catherine replied, trying to sound positive.

Joseph leaped off the boat and ran up a flight of steep steps to the top of the quay wall — and disappeared. A few minutes later he came back and signalled to Bernard.

"Don't be alarmed," Bernard's calming voice told them. "Joseph has found an empty warehouse where we can hide."

Getting Madame Barbier up the steps with no handrail and designed for nimble sailors was no easy matter.

"Take it slowly," Catherine said, looking on anxiously and hoping her companion would not slip as she plodded up the flight of slimy-wet steps.

"How horrid this is — I'm terrified of falling!" Madame Barbier puffed.

"Let's hope you do not!" Bernard retorted, who was below her expansive posterior, and in danger of toppling with her.

Although the others managed the steps more easily, and Bernard carried the baby for Gabrielle, taking the luggage up also proved difficult.

Eventually the forlorn party stood on the bleak-looking quay in front of some old buildings. Everywhere seemed deserted — Bernard said it was a good thing no-one was around.

Joseph touched his cap, saying, "Well, my friends, now I must say goodbye. It is necessary for me to catch the upstream tide."

They thanked him, and he wished them good luck. How cold it seemed.

Catherine shivered, feeling vulnerable as she watched Joseph's chaland bobbing away on the tidal water until she could see it no more — lost in the mass of shipping.

"Come along, everyone." Bernard's brisk instruction snapped her out of her reverie. He was leading them towards a dilapidated warehouse.

"I don't like the look of this place," Madame Barbier remarked.

"Nor the smell!" Gabrielle said, flaring her delicate, aristocratic nostrils.

"I'm sure we'll only be here for a short time," Catherine told them firmly.

Her task of assisting Bernard by keeping everyone's spirits up was not going to be easy. Even she was dismayed when she entered the old building and saw the filth.

"Oh, my goodness, look at the mouse droppings!"

"We can't stay here!"

"Ugh! This place stinks of rotten fish!"

Drawing in a long breath, Catherine ignored the remarks and said, "Let's get this area clean and make it as comfortable as we can, for I'm sure we'll have to spend at least one night hiding here."

She caught the quick smile of thanks Bernard sent her.

As they set to, Bernard announced that he would go and reconnoitre; find out what he could about obtaining a passage to England.

"I know this is a disagreeable place," he told them before he left, "but safety is our most important consideration, and I feel sure you will be safe here. Nevertheless, I insist you all keep out of sight by staying inside this warehouse. Nantes is crawling with fervent revolutionaries, I understand. They'll be looking for aristocrats like us. And God help us if they catch us!"

Catherine disliked the way he scared them with this brutal warning, but she knew that without Bernard's directions they would indeed be at a loss. Without his intelligence, strength and courage — and his ruthless ability to steal food — how would they manage?

Anyway, she reasoned, the first stage of their escape was over successfully. They'd soon be safely in England. However, a nagging doubt in her mind suggested their ordeal was far from over.

"Bernard should be back by now." Much later, Madame Barbier voiced the concern everyone had been feeling.

Like a dog waiting for her master's return, Violette had posted herself by the warehouse door with her plaintive eyes glued to watch along the quay. The others sat around looking dispirited — despite Catherine's efforts to distract them.

Having spent several hours cleaning up the dirty warehouse, and making it somewhat habitable, they were now all tired, yet feeling unable to relax.

"The sky is becoming overcast," Gabrielle said as she looked out of the warehouse. She cradled her baby in her arms, quietly humming a lullaby.

"Was that thunder?" Hubert started.

"I wouldn't be surprised. I've felt there's been a storm threatening for some time," Madame Barbier said reaching for her smelling salts.

Lightning flashed, followed by rumbling thunder. Rain started with slow drops, soon quickening to pelt on to the old warehouse roof and finding holes to let the water leak in. Charles began to wail. Then they heard a squawk of joy from Violette.

"Bernard's coming!" she screeched, hobbling outside to meet him, ignoring the pouring rain.

Catherine's heart leaped. She'd been more worried about Bernard than she'd wanted to admit. Excited with relief, she rushed with the others to the warehouse door to greet him. A scream outside made her gasp.

"Stay here!" she ordered the others as she pushed past them and stepped outside before Madame Barbier could stop her. She blinked at a flash of lightning, and felt the rain beating down on her. Through the murky visibility she could just make out a running figure at the end of the quay.

A musket cracked. Appalled to see some menacing forms of revolutionary guards pursuing Bernard, Catherine's fists went to her mouth to prevent herself from crying out.

Suddenly, Bernard stopped running towards the buildings and moved instead towards the edge of the quay, as though to dive into the water. Catherine knew instantly that he was trying to prevent the guards from finding them.

After another loud burst of firing she saw Bernard was hit. She watched in horror as he crumpled, tipping forward, his body fell off the high wall and into the fast-flowing Loire.

Powerless and horrified, Catherine could not move. She saw several revolutionary guards rush up to the water's edge and point their muskets down towards the water.

"I tell you I got him!" one guard yelled.

"Hurrah! That's good riddance to another of them aristos, citizens."

"Come on, let's get back and make our report — I'm soaked."

The guards' jeers and raucous boasting about how they were going to celebrate their victory with drinks at a bistro, cut into Catherine like a razor. Shivering with shock, paralysed and unable to scream, she watched with widened eyes as the guards faded away and the rain was all she heard.

Violette darted from the shadows and shrilled, "I can't see him but I know he fell here!"

Desperate, because her mind was telling her that the crippled girl was unable to act, Catherine threw off fear and ran to where Violette pointed down into the dark water.

Straining to see Bernard's body, her sobs made her breast heave painfully as she scanned the surface of the water only to see the tips of waves. He'd been swept away in the powerful Loire current. Drowned by now as his gunshot wound had made him too weak to swim.

A searing ache in her heart made Catherine cry out, "Bernard!"

"Listen!" Violette clawed at her arm.

"Catherine." A ghost of a voice from below made both girls stare into the water.

"Bernard, where are you?"

"I'm holding on to a boat ring — but can't last much longer."

Driven by urgency Catherine flew to the flight of steps and with little care for her safety stumbled down them.

"Hold on, Bernard!" she kept crying.

At the bottom she glared helplessly at the water's inky darkness. Agony smote her, knowing she was near enough to hear his voice but was unable to save him. A flash of lightning showed a small boat passing.

"Man overboard!" she screamed

at the sailors. "Search along the quayside."

Waves of icy water lapped over her bare feet — she had lost her clogs in her haste. Wind tugged and whipped her damp skirt around her legs as if wanting to drag her into the swirling current. The ominous slap of waves against the quay wall was all she heard, and she prayed the sailors had heeded her plea. She could see no sign of them, only the glimmer of lanterns from distant shipping and the shore lights from the other side of the river.

During the tortuous wait Catherine thought of Bernard's heroic sacrifice to save them all and knew if he died part of her would die, too. Then she saw a boat gliding towards her. Inside lay Bernard's limp form.

"You go up first, we'll be carrying 'im," a sailor called.

Catherine wanted to go to Bernard. Was he alive? But grateful for the sailors' help she scrambled up the steep flight of steps, and watched with pounding heart as the sure-footed sailors carried the tall man up.

Bernard's face was ashen; he was weak but alive.

"I must pay you," he said in a weak whisper. His blue lips shivered as he slipped his hand into his shirt and drew out a leather purse.

"Nay." The sailors refused, but Bernard insisted they accepted a gold piece each.

Remorse caused hot tears to slide down Catherine's cheeks. To think she'd thought Bernard had stolen food because he'd no money! She should have known he would always pay his debts.

The sailors helped Bernard inside the warehouse where Madame Barbier told Catherine and Violette to dry themselves while she undressed the injured, shivering man and wrapped him in blankets.

Bernard had a nasty shoulder wound and Madame Barbier dressed it as best she could.

"He should have the shot removed by a doctor," she said shaking her head. "The wound could fester."

"I'll go and find one," Violette piped up. "No-one will suspect me."

Without waiting for anyone to disagree she hobbled out into the night.

"Do be careful, Violette." Catherine ran after her.

"Don't you worry about me," Violette replied giving a cheeky wink.

★ ★ ★

"Catherine," Bernard murmured, reaching for her hand.

"I'm here," she said, trying to rub some warmth into his shivering body.

How she longed to ease his pain as she looked down at his haggard face. She'd never imagined him sick and vulnerable before.

"Revolutionaries!" he muttered attempting to sit up. "Don't let them find you . . . they can be brutal . . ."

"Rest now, Bernard, the guards

have gone," Catherine said soothingly, urging him to lie back.

She felt he was struggling to tell her something more, but he hadn't the strength.

The surgeon Violette managed to find rode along the quay in his buggy. He was old, very courteous — and almost deaf. Plainly dressed in a black frock-coat, he carried an ear trumpet and his medicine chest. Showing no sign of thinking it was odd for them to be there, the doctor kneeled with some difficulty to tend Bernard's wound.

Catherine watched him open his medicine chest and, taking a folded white cloth, he spread it out and laid his instruments on it.

Fortunately the competence of the surgeon was apparent. While watching the doctor's deft fingers tending the wound, Catherine hated having to restrain the patient, seeing him writhe, hearing his gasps and short cries until he became unconscious.

"He will live," the doctor said as

he stood washing his hands in the bowl of rainwater Hubert had fetched for him.

Catherine was worried in case the doctor might ask what they were doing in this dilapidated warehouse. She suspected he might know they were fugitives. But he asked no questions. He graciously accepted the small fee he asked for, telling Madame Barbier that the wound must be kept clean, and left her with some dressings.

Catherine toyed with the idea of asking his help to find a passage to England. But the doctor was so deaf it would be hopeless to try to explain their plight.

When the doctor's horse and cart had gone, Catherine surveyed the dejected faces around her. They were all sweet people but no-one was able to take Bernard's place and organise their escape from France.

"The doctor thinks Bernard will recover, so let's see if we can find something to eat," she suggested brightly.

No-one noticed she ate almost nothing as they all tucked into yesterday's loaf of bread, a sausage, some cheese and small, raw carrots. She didn't like to spoil their meal by mentioning how low their food supply had become.

The matter of finding a suitable ship to take them to England seemed to concern only her as they chatted and settled down for the night. Even Violette was now playing happily with the baby. Catherine went to check that Bernard was sleeping under the watchful eye of Madame Barbier.

Restlessly she paced the floor. It would be getting dark in a few hours. There was time for her to slip out and see if she could find that English ship they'd seen in the harbour. She told Hubert of her plan.

"I'm going to see if I can find that English ship, and ask — "

"Mais non! It is not safe for you to go out. I will go," Hubert replied.

Catherine took in a deep breath. A foppish, young aristocrat like him would soon be caught. But not wanting to say she thought him useless for the task she said, "Hubert, you are the only man able to protect us all now. You must stay here. Look, I'm well covered by this old shawl. I've lost one of my clogs so I'm going barefoot — I'll pass by the guards easily pretending to be a serving wench."

The young duc was clearly doubtful but Catherine looked at him straight in the eye.

"Hubert, something has to be done. Bernard won't be well for days. We can't stay here in this awful place for ever, now can we?"

"I don't like it. It's not right for a lady to go out unaccompanied."

"Ah, but I don't appear to be a lady, do I, Hubert?"

Seeing her confident smile, bewilderment appeared on his youthful face. Not giving him time to think of any reasons why she should not go, Catherine swept by him and turned as she walked briskly down the quay calling, "Don't worry, Hubert, I won't be long."

Ignoring the protests he sent after her, she quickly headed towards the busy harbour.

7

CATHERINE headed towards where she thought the harbour must be, keeping her drab shawl tightly held under her chin with her hand.

"Have courage," she murmured to herself as she caught sight of some revolutionary guards, and lowered her eyes as she hurried past them.

A mass of tall masts and rigging was soon to be seen silhouetted against the evening sky. She felt dwarfed by the size of these huge, ocean-going vessels. Her mission, to find a captain to take them to England, seemed a daunting task. Whatever had made her think she could succeed when Bernard had not?

Shrugging off despondency, she thought of the necessity for her errand. The others all depended on her. She must at least try to get them to safety.

She could not tolerate the idea of Bernard, and the others she loved, being imprisoned like the Marquis de Clichy.

She had walked up and back down the busy harbour, dodging the porters with their cargoes of sugar, rum and bales of cotton, hearing the sailors' raucous shouts as they climbed deftly up and down the rigging; passing by workshops where sailmakers sang sea-ditties and carpenters whistled as they sawed.

She had studied each moored ship but had not found the English schooner. She frowned, perhaps she was too late and it had already sailed. Ought she to ask if another ship was sailing to England?

She looked around wondering where she could locate the shipping office. But her eyes spied the stalls selling delicious, newly-baked pies, glistening fish and succulent hams, assorted fruits and sweetmeats. Licking her lips she found herself drawn towards the food, like the skinny urchins waiting for the spoiled goods to be thrown in the gutter. Having eaten so little for some days she felt desperately hungry, and wished she'd brought some money with her.

"What-o! Here's a pretty one!"

Catherine started. Unwittingly, she'd collided with a short, fat man. His protruding eyes and bulbous lips gave the impression of a man used to indulging himself. His striped trousers had a wide, dark sash around his rotund waist; his bicorne hat sported a red, white and blue cockade. A revolutionary!

Catherine's eyes and mouth shot open as she backed away, but too late. He grasped her wrist like an iron bracelet.

"Get off, you dog!" she cried, remembering to shout like a peasant.

"Ho, citizens see what I've caught!" the guard crowed. "This one has spirit — I like 'em with spirit."

Trying to pull away, Catherine

released her grip on her head shawl so that tendrils of her hair escaped. Immediately her shawl was yanked away.

"We've found a right good 'un here, citizens." A greasy hand was mauling her abundant dark hair, and Catherine felt sick in the stomach. She cried out to be set free. The crowd milling around ignored her cries.

Stunned by their indifference, her cheeks flamed — too late she realised that men seeing a young woman hanging around the harbour alone at night would expect her to be a harlot! Catherine's slight body offered little resistance as the guards dragged and prodded her along with them.

"Let me go," she sobbed.

The thought of the horror of being molested by them made her mouth dry with fear. Desperately she tried to think of something she could do to prevent these animals having their way with her. Despair engulfed her.

Sharp as a knife a shrill voice came

from a pile of rags in the dark alley they were taking from the harbour.

One of the guards called back, "Not tonight, old hag — our pleasure is arranged." The other guffawed.

"A gipsy's fortune-telling should not be spurned — it'll bring you bad luck, citizens."

There was something about that voice . . . The guards, uncertain, slowed. One dug his hand into his pocket.

"Here, take that."

The sound of a coin tinkling on the cobbles was followed by the insistent shrill again.

"Your fortunes — or a curse on you, citizens."

One guard was uneasy.

"I know a man who was ruined by a gipsy's curse," one said in a hushed voice. "He injured his hand so bad he lost his job as a cobbler."

As the men began to argue, Catherine felt a kick on her shin and saw the bundle of rags had moved towards her.

"Run for your life, Catherine," Violette urged.

Staggered to discover the gipsy was Violette, Catherine hesitated only a moment before twisting her wrist from the man's grasp, and jumping aside as he tried to grab her again. Foul curses sounded behind her as she fled.

"Don't you worry your heads about her, citizens. Let her go." Violette's gipsy voice shrilled above the guards' howls of rage. "There's aplenty more girls like her to be had down at the harbour."

Running until she was breathless, Catherine had no idea where she was going. Enclosed by mean streets which were uninviting and evil-smelling, she became lost in a squalid maze

Exhausted, she had to stop running. Gasping for breath she listened for sounds of the guards pursuing her. But she heard nothing but a coarse woman's scolding voice resounding from one of the hovels.

She put her hand to her hot forehead,

shaken with fright still. She had got away — with Violette's assistance. She waited in case Violette should come looking for her.

But after a while she realised she was waiting in vain — the maid would not know which way she'd run. And knowing Violette to be canny, Catherine reasoned the little maid would be able to look after herself. She must find the harbour and get back to the warehouse.

It had become quite dark now. Lost and tired she wandered down one dreary lane and then another.

Scared of every little noise, afraid of shadows, frustrated not to be able to find the harbour, tears threatened. She wiped them from her face with the back of her hand.

Things could be worse. At the moment she was free, she was not injured like Bernard. She only had to find the way to the others. Resolutely she set off again.

The bright lights of an inn attracted

her. Perhaps she could ask someone the way. As she approached, ribald laughter and lusty shouts from within the tavern made Catherine pause. Would it be safer to pass by this den of drinkers?

"Where are you going, my pretty?" A drunken sailor barred her way.

Aware of the new danger she was facing, Catherine cried out in fear and exasperation.

"Let me pass you drunken brute!" Unwittingly, she spoke in English!

"Egad, Johnathan, I swear I heard an English voice — a lady, too, I'll warrant."

Surprised, Catherine turned to see a couple of frock-coated gentlemen behind her.

"I'm very pleased to meet you," she said sincerely, gasping with relief as she saw the sailor sidle off.

"You are alone, I see." The taller Englishman, whose face was lined and ruddy, but not lecherous, looked down steadily at her.

"Well, I . . . am at the moment."

His smile was shrewd.

"Begging your pardon, ma'am, it is quite plain to us, and I daresay it would be to others, that your attire belies your speech." He lowered his head to whisper in her ear. "You are in some kind of trouble, are you not?".

Catherine's mouth felt dry. She was at her wits' end. What point was there to lie to this Englishman when she needed his help?

"Yes, I am," she croaked.

"In what way can I help?"

"I'm looking for a ship . . . " It was the truth, but in the present circumstances it sounded incongruous, and Catherine gave him a wry smile.

The man looked at his companion as his lips twitched.

"Hum. Do you wish to leave France, young lady?"

"Oh, yes, indeed I do."

"Have you any money?"

"Why, yes, sir. But not with me. I should have to ask Madame Barb . . . Oh, dear!"

What about the others? And Bernard lying sick. She would certainly go nowhere without him. The two men were exchanging glances again.

"Well, now, I suggest we step into the inn, ma'am and over some refreshment we can discuss . . . our arrangements, eh?"

Catherine had no choice but to take a chance with them. At least they'd presented her with some hope. A whiff of delicious cooking from the inn kitchens made her feel weak with hunger.

If the taller gentleman hadn't a certain air of command about him, and his friend a look that would make anyone think twice before tackling him, Catherine felt she would not have remained inside the inn.

She was shocked to see the place was most disreputable, filled with brawling, rough-looking men.

Her heart raced as in the candlelight she saw girls lolling over sailors who were drinking too much. Roars were coming from a corner of the tavern where some form of boisterous entertainment was amusing the wild and merry crowd.

Fortunately she was quickly escorted to a high-backed, wooden bench in a quieter corner. Mouth-watering smells from the kitchen alongside made Catherine look to see a lively fire burning, with a roast sizzling on the spit. A bellied, copper pot gave off a delectable aroma of pottage which drew her eyes to fix on it.

"We usually take our dinner here. Perhaps you would care for a platter, ma'am?"

"I certainly would," Catherine answered with a lamentable lack of reticence that Madame Barbier would have chided her for.

The serving man was promptly called for, and the order given. Food had never tasted so good.

Catherine enjoyed eggs in a creamy, cheese sauce, followed by roasted chicken, and then fruit pastries, eaten with gusto — and deplorable table manners she would be ashamed to admit to later.

Her wine glass was replenished as she sat back and became aware of the men eyeing her.

"So now to business, Miss . . . ?"

Colour rose in Catherine's cheeks.

"I don't know if I should tell you my name," she said, wishing she did not have to think of serious matters after such a delicious meal.

"Come, come, ma'am, we are Englishmen — you need hide nothing from us. You are used to wearing silk, are you not? So it stands to reason you are disguised for some purpose — having a spot of trouble with the new revolutionary régime, eh?"

"You are right. But we — oh!"

"Ah! Your family is in trouble, too?"

Catherine shook her head.

"No, not my family. My friends, sir."

"Intriguing, ma'am. Tell us more."

She took a deep breath as she surveyed the men. They didn't look as if they were rogues. She didn't want to betray her friends but realised she had to take a risk. Briefly she explained their plight.

"So your father is the Earl of Shendish. Yes, I do believe I may have met him. He runs a fine estate near Frome."

Catherine's eyes sparkled. Any man who knew her father must be trustworthy. There was a pause as the men conferred, and Catherine's heart thudded so loudly she thought they might hear it. Their conference over, they faced her again.

"Now, Lady Catherine, you have told us who you are and so let us introduce ourselves. I am Captain Blair, and this is my mate, Mr Johnathan Woodward. We do a little business . . . with the French. My schooner, The Penrose, is in the harbour. If you are willing to sign a promise that your father will pay me for the passage, I'm prepared to take all of you to England tomorrow."

Catherine took a deep breath in and expelled it with great satisfaction.

Her wide, dimpled smile gave him his answer.

Captain Blair called for some paper, quill and ink, and prepared a pledge which Catherine signed.

The captain paid the tavern's bill, saying that if it pleased her, it would be put on her account.

It seemed most businesslike, and Catherine agreed. The officers gallantly escorted her back to the warehouse.

She was embarrassed to let them see the desperate conditions they were living in, so she stopped them outside.

"It's late, and my friends are all sleeping, Captain Blair. So I won't ask you in to meet them."

The officers both inclined their heads, murmuring they quite understood, and would look forward to meeting everyone tomorrow. Removing his tricorne, the captain wished her good-night, and assured her he would send the jolly boat alongside in the morning to pick them up.

Catherine went into the warehouse

feeling a lot happier about her situation than she had done earlier that evening.

The flame on the candle Madame Barbier held almost held out as she scolded.

"Catherine, where have you been? I've been so worried about you."

But her temper was contradicted as she gave Catherine a bear hug, showing she was more scared for her than angry.

"I've some good news, Madame Barbier. I've arranged our passage to England on an English schooner — tomorrow morning a boat will come to the quay to pick us up."

Madame Barbier's eyes almost popped out.

"Oh, Catherine, you are incredible!"

"Now tell me, Madame Barbier, how's Bernard?"

"He slept soundly, and although he's sore, I think he's over the worst. Bernard's a healthy, young man and should heal quickly."

Catherine felt her heart leap and

twirled around on her toes giving little cries of joy.

"Hush, ma cherie, you'll wake everyone. Go to Bernard, he's been asking after you. I've been making all kinds of excuses as to why you were not able to see him earlier. Here, take this candle, try to get him to sleep again."

She yawned.

"I'm going to bed, I could hardly keep my eyes open waiting for you." She yawned again.

Catherine kissed her faithful companion good-night. Noting a hump where Violette slept, Catherine was thankful the maid had arrived back safely. She did not like to disturb the girl's sleep by going over to thank her.

★ ★ ★

She stood lighting up the sick man with her candle. His eyes were closed, his noble features drained. Despite what Madame Barbier said, Catherine thought he looked no better. She fell on her knees beside him, placing the candle near his face, her hand stroking his head gently. In the flickering light his eyelids opened slowly.

"Catherine," he murmured as if in pain. "Is it you?"

He grasped her hand with such vigour she knew he must be mending.

"How are you, Bernard?" she asked.

"I would rather not say how I feel. But certainly better for seeing you. Where have you been?"

Catherine's fingers passed gently over his brow, and without thinking of the propriety of her actions, she stooped to kiss his pale lips lightly.

He smiled as he tried weakly to respond.

"I've arranged our passage to England," she said quickly, keen to tell him the good news.

He made to rise and groaned as he said, "Good God, Catherine, don't tease me. Surely you can see I'm not in any fit state for jokes."

"But I'm not teasing or joking. It's the truth."

His grey-lined eyes fixed on hers.

"Do you mean to tell me you've managed to — "

"Book us a passage? Yes." She nodded. "Tomorrow morning Captain Blair of the English schooner will be sending his jolly boat to collect us."

He winced with pain as he moved to rise and she restrained him with a smile on her face.

"You see, you are not the only capable person here, my lord. Hoydenish English ladies don't just sit around with their embroidery all day long! We go for the high fences!"

His face took on a comical expression as if to appear chastised.

"I take back all I said about them."

Her face dimpled as she said, "You must go to sleep now, Bernard."

He took her hand and, turning it, pressed his lips on her palm, sending shivers of delight through her.

"God bless you, Catherine." He was

exhausted and immediately closed his eyes.

She tucked his blanket around him, smoothed his hair in place and lightly kissed his forehead.

"Sleep well, my love," she murmured picking up the candle.

Catherine felt she was too overwrought to sleep worrying about the morrow — what if anything should go wrong. Yet she fell asleep the moment she wrapped herself in a blanket and lay down by Madame Barbier on the hard floor of the warehouse.

★ ★ ★

The baby was grizzling. Having been such a contented child during the sunny river journey, he was now objecting to being cooped up in the gloomy building.

In particular, young Charles was voicing everyone's concern . . . his nursemaid was missing!

Catherine sat up stretching, and

yawned, then rubbed her eyes. She heard Madame Barbier's voice.

"I tell you, Violette has tricked us," she was saying. "Look, she made this pile of clothes so that we would think it was her sleeping — now why would she do that?"

Catherine was too stunned to speak as she recollected the previous evenings's events.

Violette had saved her — but had the little, crippled girl been captured by the revolutionary guards? She shuddered to think what had nearly been her fate.

Guilt made Catherine shut her eyes. Should she own up to what had happened last night, or would it only make the party more distressed than they already were? She decided that she — as Bernard had — should keep as much worry as she could from the others.

She called out, "Don't fret about Violette. She is French — and an orphan well able to take care of herself." Making the effort to smile until their sad faces lit up she added, "Now, get your things together because we are being collected by boat this morning. As Madame Barbier has probably already told you, we are sailing to England on the English schooner we saw in the harbour."

In their activity Violette was forgotten, though for Catherine the burden of worry about the maid's safety weighed like lead. Her anxiety increased as each minute went by. What would she do if the English boat came and Violette had not returned?

Madame Barbier was attending to Bernard.

"He's still sleeping. Leave him. Rest is the best thing for him."

Without Bernard's strength it took them all some time to move their luggage to the warehouse door.

But having done it, they were listless after their exertions, and remembering Violette was missing, they sat in a glum group trying to guess what had become of her.

Catherine paced the floor, clenching her fists. What had happened to the girl? The boat was due to collect them at any time. Should she get the others on to it and stay behind? What would I do if I did, she asked herself. Oh, dear God, let Violette come before the boat arrives!

"Bernard is awake. He says he's feeling much better." Madame Barbier's voice lifted everyone's spirits and the party crowded around his pallet.

"I can't pretend my arm doesn't hurt me — I don't suppose you'd believe me if I told you it didn't." Bernard grinned at their relieved faces.

His eyes sought for Catherine's, and he gave her a private smile which for a moment evaporated her tension. He was indeed greatly recovered.

He wanted to know more about the arrangements Catherine had made, and began to question her. She found he accepted her now as an equal and it was easy to talk to him as to a friend.

"I just hope Captain Blair keeps his word," she said, putting her finger over her mouth, thinking belatedly that she had no copy of the pledge she had signed.

"Indeed, so do I," Bernard said with a touch of humour in his smile. He leaned forward to pat her hand. "Never mind, my dear Catherine, you did well, and we won't look for any faults in your arrangements."

As their attention was clearly on each other, the others drifted away to leave them alone. But Catherine sensed Bernard was already tiring so she didn't like to admit she had many reservations.

As she stared at him she felt tears welling in her eyes.

"Anyone here hungry?" A shrill voice sounded from the doorway and they turned to see Violette's little figure. She was carrying a basket half her size, covered with a white cloth!

"Violette! Oh, Violette!" Catherine was the first to dart to her and embrace her with a kiss on both cheeks.

"You can't have been worried about me!"

The joy glowed on the crippled girl's face as everyone made a fuss of her. Then there were cries of amazement when Violette drew back the basket's cover to reveal a sumptuous array: cream cheeses, capons, fresh bread rolls, a tin can of milk and some bottles of wine.

Catherine's eyes brimmed with tears.

"Violette, you are wonderful!"

"And I've got a special bottle of Muscadet for my lord Bernard — that should put him on his feet again!"

"Bernard is feeling much better, Violette. Although still pained and weak from his injury."

As the food was being distributed and eaten, Catherine came to sit by Violette.

"What happened to you?" she whispered.

Violette chuckled.

"Well, after you ran off, I had to

pacify them revolutionary guards, so I says to them, seeing as you lost the wench, I'll tell your fortunes for nothing."

Violette took a bite from her capon. "Well, they took me to their bistro and I asked them to find some tarot cards — you see my grandmother taught me divining."

A mischievous glint showed on her little face as she related some of the things she'd said.

"Oh, Violette, I can't believe you had the nerve!" Catherine laughed, almost choking at her impudence.

"I did. I can assure you I got my own back on them guards. More and more of 'em kept coming to have their fortunes told though. So I didn't get away until early this morning. Anyways, some paid me — more money than I've ever had in me life!"

"And you spent that money on getting us food? Violette, you are a dear, little minx!"

"Well, you and Bernard, and everyone

else, have all been kind to me. Besides, French money ain't much use in England, is it? Anyways we needed food to fill our empty bellies, didn't we?"

Looking around at the contented munching going on, Catherine had to agree. She began to tell Violette about what had happened to her when they parted.

There was a jovial atmosphere after they'd all eaten. They were taken by surprise when they heard a call and the patter of bare feet outside.

"Ahoy, there!"

A sailor ran into the warehouse asking in a Cornish accent, "Be this the party for The Penrose?"

"Yes," Catherine answered boldly as she stood to answer him, willing herself to appear unruffled, yet apprehensive of what she had let everyone in for.

"Get yourselves moving into the jolly boat, missy, the tide'll be turning afore long."

8

AS the schooner Penrose set sail from Nantes harbour that afternoon, Catherine felt she should be elated. They had escaped from the turmoil the Revolution had begun to bring to France, but she sensed other difficulties.

What would she say to her stern father when she arrived home with five French emigrés — plus a baby?

However, she had plenty of time to think over that problem, or at least as long as it took them to reach England.

Captain Blair had kept his word so far. Their accommodation on board was roomier than it had been on the river barge. They were being fed and treated courteously by the crew.

Bernard's tall, lean figure, she noticed, matched Captain Blair's, and their ability to command was similar, too. Catherine detected an instinctive rivalry as they met, and hoped nothing would put them at odds.

That evening, she noticed Bernard standing for hours under an oil lamp that swayed in the gimbals, throwing patterns of light and dark shadows over his harsh-set features.

His sombre eyes and compressed mouth revealed to no-one but her what mental torment he must be suffering.

He must be worrying about his imprisoned father. Thankfully his mother was long dead — like her own — and he was not having to think of her suffering in prison, too.

Bernard would be wondering about his future in England. A French nobleman without land — or the horses he loved. She could not imagine a proud man like Bernard content to work as a stable boy!

As Madame Barbier had told her, he would not be driven to do anything. What she did not know was that he was also wrestling with his feelings about her. He scowled as he looked down into the churning sea, grasping the bulwarks tightly.

His injury gave him torment. The last thing he had expected, with all his other things that had upset his life, was to fall in love with Catherine. She was lovely, but so young . . .

Fate had thrust them together, but he knew he should not encourage their love when he was not in the position to offer her security. He had to return to France to try to rescue his father when he had delivered Catherine safely to her father.

And he may not get out of that venture alive, and even if he did, he still had to make a new life for himself in England . . . as a foreigner.

A sob of acute loss caught his breath as the pulling power of the wind increased, and the schooner, with full sails, moved at a good pace out of the Loire estuary and out into the open sea. Sheer exhaustion sent everyone to sleep that night. The ship's rhythmic movement was soothing as the brig ploughed through the seas.

★ ★ ★

The others were already up and about when Catherine rose next day. Sunlight streamed in through the vessel's small portholes. She could see they were sailing smoothly towards England in a fresh wind.

Gurgles and laughter came from baby Charles, as Violette's chirpy chatter amused him. The sound of French voices made Catherine think it was time to remind them to start speaking in English. Madame Barbier, having lived in England for some years, spoke it well. Bernard, she discovered, had a surprisingly good command of the language. She supposed he had been well taught by his tutor as a boy.

The Duc and Duchess had mastered only a small amount of the English language and would need her help to learn more. Violette, of course, knew none. But Catherine knew Violette was crafty enough to manage even if she could not speak a word!

"Isn't it wonderful to be able to wear our own clothes again?" Catherine twirled around in her flower-printed cotton gown, and then stood to admire Gabrielle's.

"It is . . . what you say? Magnifique . . . to wear our leather shoes," Gabrielle said, dancing on tiptoe as though she were at a court ball.

"Marvellous," Catherine corrected with a smile at the elegant French lady.

"It is so agreeable not to have to worry every minute that some revolutionary guards might suddenly appear and toss one of us into prison," Madame Barbier said as she brought the young ladies cups of steaming hot coffee.

Catherine beamed, happy to see everyone bubbling with good humour. She was well aware though, that

Bernard did not share their happiness. He was up and dressed — although how he'd managed it with his injured shoulder she was not sure. He had given her no more than a cursory greeting, and was stalking around the ship like a cat after a bird.

And when she overheard snatches of conversation that sounded more like a heated argument between the Captain and His Lordship, she became uneasy. As soon as she was able to catch him alone on deck, she picked up her skirts and rushed to speak to him.

"Bernard, I . . . "

She held her breath as he turned to gaze at her.

He looked so devastatingly handsome, attired in his well-tailored travel coat and breeches — and although his arm was in a sling, he still possessed an aura of male strength and elegance which made her feel feminine and vulnerable.

"Bernard . . . " she began again, wondering if she should be calling him My Lord. He had not only cast aside his peasant clothes but appeared to have adopted a formidable lordly attitude. "I was wondering what has caused you to be so irritated with Captain Blair." Her lifted eyes met his sardonic smile.

"This," he said, producing a piece of paper.

"What is it?"

"You don't recognise it, Lady Catherine? You signed it."

She was surprised to see it was the written agreement she had made with Captain Blair.

He suddenly began to tear it up into pieces and allowed the bits to be blown away into the sea. Catherine looked up at him with wide, puzzled eyes.

"Why did you do that? It was my promise to pay the captain for our passage — I mean, my father will pay him."

"How much?"

"Well, he didn't say." Colour rose to her cheeks. "I thought he would know what was a fair price."

Bernard's direct gaze made her uncomfortable.

"My dear Catherine, Captain Blair is a scoundrel."

"How do you know?" she stammered fearfully.

"I took a stroll around the ship earlier, and can you guess what I found stored in the hold?"

"No, I can't, tell me." Catherine held on tightly to a guy rope.

"Contraband," he declared. "Your Captain Blair is a smuggler."

Catherine swallowed. Then she murmured, "I could name worse things." Her body relaxed as she began to breathe normally again.

Bernard looked amused and gave a short laugh.

"Just so, ma'am. However, it will be better for us if we are not caught by an English excise ship."

She felt he was treating her as an inferior, as he used to, and wondered why he was no longer the close friend she had known during their escape from France.

She loved him deeply, and had thought he loved her, but now a demon of doubt had appeared. Surely Bernard was not a heartless man who played with ladies feelings when it suited him?

"So," she said, choked with disappointment, and furious he'd found fault with her arrangement with the captain, "you think Captain Blair will overcharge my father?"

"No. I struck a bargain with him. He agreed he would only charge a reasonable fare — and gave me your pledge — and we, in return, would not reveal his illegal trade to customs."

She had to smile. He'd done it again, outwitted her. Was it surprising he thought her a ninnyhammer still? But it hurt to think that he had decided not to continue their intimate relationship. Perhaps she could entice him back?

Her smile of resolve made her dimples show, and her eyes twinkled as she looked up challengingly at him.

"That sounds fair, my lord."

No, it is not fair, he thought, not able to prevent himself from laughing at her flirtatious expression — although it made both his heart and his wound hurt. It was going to be so difficult for him to pretend he did not love her . . .

"I think Madame Barbier is waiting to change my dressing, if you will excuse me, Catherine," he said giving her a formal bow, and resisting the urge to kiss her rosy lips.

★ ★ ★

She found it impossible to talk to him again. It was as though he was trying to avoid her. And remembering she had treated him in the same manner when she'd thought he'd been stealing, she really couldn't believe his coolness was because he didn't care for her, she decided there must be some other reason for his change in attitude towards her.

The following day there was excitement in the French party as they could see the coast of Cornwall as the schooner sailed towards Falmouth harbour.

Catherine noted Bernard was joking with Captain Blair, leaving Mr Woodward to shout instructions at the crew. Before long the wind took the sails' canvas so that the ship was able to sail majestically into Falmouth harbour.

Catherine closed her eyes saying a prayer of thanks they'd arrived safely. Then she gazed at Pendennis Castle; the panorama of distant green fields, the trees and grazing cattle, and admired the town's clean-looking, grey-slated buildings.

After she'd thanked Captain Blair, she stepped down the gang plank. It felt so good to be back in England. She looked around to make sure everyone and their luggage was taken off the ship.

Falmouth harbour was thriving; mail packets sailed to distant lands from there. As Bernard's attention focused on four magnificent Cleveland Bay coach horses harnessed to the mail coach, and he went over to admire them, the rest of them were left, being stared at by the locals.

"I don't like standing here being gawped at," Madame Barbier said to Catherine. "We may be foreigners to them — but we are not a side show!"

"I suppose we'd better get a porter to take our luggage to the posting inn, so that we can take the stage. May I have some English money, Madame Barbier?"

Catherine looked aghast at Madame Barbier's meagre collection of six guineas and three gold crowns, plus a few shillings and pennies.

"Is that all you have?"

"What do you expect? I'm not a bank!"

Catherine became worried. How was she going to transfer everyone to Frome in Somerset on six guineas? There were the stage-coach fares to pay, and every forty miles, lodging, meals and tolls.

She decided the best thing would be to find cheap lodgings and send an express letter to her father asking him to send her more money. Porters were hailed to cart the luggage, and they all trudged after them to the posting inn.

Catherine did not like the look of the shabby building, nor the landlord whose burly figure had a stained apron tied around it. But she managed to pluck up the courage.

"We would like to stay here for a few days," she began, aware of him glaring over her shoulder at the French party behind her. "I will pay you when my father sends me some money."

"French refugees, eh?" he interrupted her loudly with a smirk on his thick lips. "Got a spot of bother over in France so them Frenchies come flocking over 'ere, without a penny between them. This lot's come down in the world, ain't they?"

His sneering face made Catherine cringe and she felt embarrassed that her French friends had come to face such gross English hostility.

She opened her mouth to say as much, but the landlord continued, "Well, now, Frenchies, I dare say I can find you dishes to wash, and plenty of floors to scrub for your bread."

"That won't be necessary, landlord!" Bernard's voice cut through his coarse laughter, effectively taking the wind out of the landlord's sails. Bernard turned to the party. "I've found us a superior inn."

The landlord's manner changed abruptly, seeing Bernard's commanding figure. He mumbled that his best rooms were available, but Bernard did not even thank him as he ushered the party outside.

Catherine was thankful Bernard had appeared to bail them out of the nasty situation. However, she quaked to think of the cost of the superior inn he had found.

"Bernard," she whispered urgently

taking his arm, "we have only six guineas."

He looked mildly puzzled and she frowned as she gazed up at him.

"We can't afford anything expensive . . . I will have to request my father to send us some money."

"Damn it, I will pay."

"Bernard, they will not accept livres — "

"My dear Catherine, I have plenty of English money with me."

Her frown faded as her mouth curved into a smile. She might have known Bernard would have everything under control. It was a nice feeling to know she did not have to worry about the finances any more.

However, it struck her that there was something a bit too cocksure about Bernard's manner. He did not seem in the least put out about being in England. On the contrary, he was perfectly at ease.

"You are all welcome," the new innkeeper said, while his wife showed she was keen to make their customers comfortable.

"This is much better than the other place," Madame Barbier puffed. She had become quite out-of-breath climbing the short hill to the inn. Both she and Catherine looked around their clean bedchamber with approval.

Their well-cooked evening meal was appreciated by everyone. Violette tended the baby, putting him to bed, and soon after, they all retired, except for Bernard who had consumed a goodly quantity of first class jugged hare, and was now enjoying a tankard of the best English ale, in their private parlour.

Catherine hesitated before she climbed the stairs. Then she swept back into the parlour thinking this was a good time to speak to Bernard alone. She had the excuse to warn him about his arrogant manner, which might upset her father.

When she opened the door and spied the assured gentleman, the prospect of cautioning him made her apprehensive.

"Ah, Catherine, I thought you'd gone to bed." He rose politely. Was he pleased to see her? She detected he was — and yet he seemed to be on his guard.

"Am I disturbing you, Bernard?"

"Not at all. Take a seat."

As she did, her planned speech deserted her mind. An awkward silence made them both look at the crackling parlour fire.

"Does your arm ache, Bernard?" Catherine asked.

"Not over much," he replied, sipping his beer.

Catherine sat stiffly on the bench facing him with a pensive expression on her face.

"Bernard, I have something to say that is, difficult for me to express."

He put his tankard down on the table and sat up, giving her his full attention.

"You see, I do not wish to upset you."

He looked faintly surprised.

"You can say anything you like to me, my dear," he said softly, his concerned face making her heart flutter.

She wished she could ask him outright why he was being so distant as she looked down at her lap, twisting her fingers.

Instead she said, "Let me explain that my father is not an easy man to get on with. He has been withdrawn from society ever since my mama died. In fact, my brothers and I feel he is so full of anger at times, we hardly dare approach him."

She flicked her eyelashes upwards to see how he was taking this admission. He seemed fractionally amused, which annoyed her.

"You are not taking me seriously, I think."

"Indeed I am, Catherine."

"You will not think it amusing when my father calls you a top-lofty French pauper!" she said rudely, the truth of her message tumbling out before she'd considered her words. She immediately went bright pink.

"The Earl of Shendish sounds a regular Trojan!"

"You will soon find out that he is!" she said, becoming furious that he appeared not to be in the slightest abashed by her warning.

Seeing he had upset her, he rose and came to sit by her. She turned her head away from him in a manner which made Bernard want to embrace her.

"Forgive me, my love. I'm aware of my sin of pride. You are quite right to remind me that now I have been dispossessed, and have nothing — "

Remorse struck Catherine, bringing tears to her eyes. She looked round at him.

"Oh, I did not mean to add to your misery!"

Bernard placed his finger under her chin and raised it, placing a firm kiss on her trembling mouth.

"I know what you are trying to tell me, and your concern for my welfare has not gone unnoticed."

She felt confused. Did he really understand how much she loved her French friends, and was worried her father might not? Did Bernard know that she loved him most of all; and that he was the one most likely to upset her father? If he did, he was taking pains not to show it.

"Catherine, I don't wish you to concern yourself over me. When you get home, learn to be a carefree, young lady of fashion again. Have fun and play with your young friends. Then you will find the man you wish to marry."

But she already had found the man she wished to marry! She looked deeply into his sad eyes for a sign that he knew it, too.

But his expression gave nothing away. Did he really mean what he said: he did not want her?

Her face became bathed in tears as she said, "But, I want — "

"No! You can't choose until you've

had a choice, Catherine," he said firmly, yet tenderly gazing at her troubled face and putting his good arm around her. He drew her sobbing body towards him.

Feeling the warmth of his strong hand stroking her shoulders, she clung to him, burying her head in the crisp whiteness of his neckcloth and knew she wanted to be with him for ever.

After a few minutes, when his instinct was to give in to her heartfelt sobs, his breath caressed her hair.

"You are tired Catherine — it's a reaction to all you've been through recently. You've been a brave girl. I am indebted to you and will tell your father. Now you must go to bed."

Gently easing her away from him, he stood, and walked to the parlour door, opening it for her.

"It's late. You need your rest, now off you go."

As she passed him, he stopped her with his hand.

"Time will heal our sufferings," he

161

said quietly, stooping to kiss her forehead. "You'll see."

Catherine gazed up at the man she loved, feeling he was trying to tell her to be patient.

Content with that hope, she gave him a hesitant smile, which he rewarded with one of his broad, attractive grins.

9

THEIR journey to Frome, Catherine thought, was reminiscent of their journey down the Loire, because, as they were a large party, Bernard had hired a private coach.

He travelled outside with the coachman, and to her surprise seemed to be interested in mastering the driving. All signs of his injury seemed to have vanished when he took the reins.

He appeared to have few cares in the world as he chatted in a friendly fashion to the coachman.

And when Catherine asked him what he found to talk about, Bernard said that they shared a love of horses and the countryside.

Naturally Catherine was pleased to see him content in England, but she would have liked him to sit by her. The memory of the tender way he'd held her the night before, and his gentle kisses, made her heart throb and her cheeks flush. The new passion she felt for him was both frightening and exciting.

★ ★ ★

During the long days of travelling from Falmouth to Truro, up over the moors of Bodmin, through Exeter and Taunton, she was left to mull over what she was going to say to her father, as stage by stage they came nearer her home. Increasingly she feared the French people she was bringing back with her would look a poor investment as far as her father was concerned.

A proud French nobleman — with no property; an impoverished young duc and his elegant wife and their baby; a crippled peasant maid who could not speak English, and her stout, sometimes excitable companion. Her father was bound to ask her what use they were to him if he housed and fed them all!

"I'm weary of this interminable journey," Madame Barbier exclaimed. "I'll be so glad when we arrive, and do not have to suffer being thrown about in a coach all day long."

Catherine looked at her sympathetically.

"You do look fatigued, Madame Barbier. But I'm certain it won't be long now before we get to Lance Court."

"Thank goodness for that!"

A murmur of agreement sounded within the coach. The carriage had been bumping and lurching along the West Country roads for several days.

Catherine said, "Yes, I'm sure we've changed the horses for the last time." Then to give them something to anticipate she suggested, "Look out for the big, wrought-iron gates as we enter the park."

Before long they were bowling down the drive and Catherine was thrilled to see the familiar three-storeyed mansion that was her home. It hadn't the grandeur of the beautiful chateaux she had admired in France, but it was impressive, and imposingly set in the green Somerset countryside.

Soon the coach swung along the wide avenue edged with lime trees. The horses hooves clattered over the bridge where the lake shone like a silver ribbon in front of the entrance to the big house.

Everyone was eager to arrive — except for Catherine who had mixed feelings as she began to rehearse what she would say to her father.

Later she nervously entered her father's fine library.

The Earl of Shendish, wearing an old-fashioned periwig and a bottle green suit, sat at his curved, mahogany writing table.

This book-lined room was his retreat. Ever since his young wife had died in child-bed, he'd spent most of his time there rarely seeing his two sons and daughter, who were placed in the care of nurses and tutors.

Apprehensively, Catherine stood waiting for him to notice her. She felt a sudden wave of empathy for this lonely, old man, and wondered fleetingly if her love for Bernard had opened her heart to a greater understanding of her father.

"Papa."

He turned, expressing pleasure to see her.

"Why, Catherine, my dearest child," he said, rising and coming towards her, "I hardly recognise you . . . you are much changed. Why, you have become quite as beautiful as your mama was."

She'd rarely seen his tender smile. She realised it was because she'd been usually hauled before him to be reprimanded for some childish misdeed — and she'd been guilty of taking part in many of her brothers' pranks. His display of affection made it easy for her to embrace him warmly.

"After reading the newspaper accounts of the Revolution in France, I feared for your safety."

She was astonished to hear him say that he had been thinking about her and was concerned for her safety.

She resisted an urge to weep, to pour out an account of her sufferings. Her newly-acquired maturity made her diplomatic.

She merely said, "We did have a few awkward moments, Papa."

Her warm, dimpled smile, her elegant French clothes, her deportment and manners, enchanted him.

"Come and tell me of your adventures," he said, indicating he wanted her to stay with him awhile.

Tactfully, Catherine wove in a description of the French party as she related her story, entertaining him with her lively account — and occasionally making him laugh. His interest aroused, his daughter requested he summon the butler to ask her French friends to make an appearance.

★ ★ ★

"Madame Barbier." The Earl greeted her warmly. "I have much to thank you for. When my daughter left England she was far too spirited a filly — "

Madame Barbier, who'd had time to wash away the travel dust and take some refreshment, interrupted him.

"My Lord, I've always regarded your daughter's liveliness to be admirable. She has always been a most dear child to me. I regret she was unable to enjoy more time in France."

Approving her little speech, the earl smiled as he nodded.

"Madame, the time you were able to spend there has been most beneficial. You have turned Catherine into a charming, young lady."

Catherine saw the opportunity and interjected.

"Papa, I would like Madame Barbier

to remain as my companion, but considering her advanced years, perhaps you will allow her to take things a little easier — and allow her a small pension?"

She held her breath as the earl considered this proposition.

"Indeed." He turned to the older French lady. "Your presence and conversation in this house has been missed, madame." He winked at her. "Promise me you'll stroll around the lake, and play piquet of an evening, and I'll be glad of your companionship myself, Marie."

Madame Barbier's hands fluttered; her chins wobbled as she almost cried with delight. Then the young Duc de Verry moved forward and bowed elegantly. His wife curtsied prettily in the correct French court manner.

"Papa, Hubert is a most talented violinist. He has enchanted us with his playing. I'm sure he is able to give musical concerts to polite society in Bath. And his wife, Gabrielle, has given me advice with my dress and deportment. I'm sure she would be much in demand to instruct young girls. Ladies in this country are most anxious to have their daughters taught the social graces today."

The earl nodded and rubbed his chin. Catherine tensed, waiting for his verdict. At last he spoke.

"Well, now, the Dower House is at present unoccupied. If the Duc and Duchesse and their young son would like to make use of it — "

"Papa, thank you. I know they would. And little Violette here — who saved me as I explained to you — could live there, too, and be Charles's nursemaid.

Smiles all round told Catherine that her plans for them all were working far better than she had expected. But her heart beat faster as Bernard was introduced.

How proudly he stood facing her father. Her acute anxiety made her tremble. Seeing the two men she loved look challengingly at each other, she longed to rush to Bernard's side, to plead for her father to disregard his high-handed attitude, and assure him of Bernard's true worth.

"Your servant, My Lord," Bernard broke the silence at last, bowing formally.

"My good fellow," the earl said, "I believe it is you I have to thank for bringing my daughter back to me safely."

"I think Catherine is to be congratulated, my lord. But for her courage we would be still stuck in Nantes."

Catherine felt her cheeks burn as everyone clapped and murmured their approval.

Her heart felt like bursting as her father took her hand and whispered, "Indeed, I am proud of you, daughter."

He then turned to speak to Bernard.

"And what news of your father, the Marquis de Clichy?"

Bernard's expression hardened.

"Now that I have completed my duty

to see Catherine into your hands, sir, I must return and discover my father's whereabouts — and help him if I possibly can."

A hammer blow of dismay hit Catherine. She felt like screaming. No! It was far too dangerous for Bernard to return to France. He would be caught and cast into prison like his father.

But this was not the time to reveal that she knew the marquis was condemned to the discomforts and indignities of a Paris gaol, held there by the French revolutionaries not for a crime he had committed, but merely because he was an aristocrat.

Nor should she try to prevent a loving son from trying to save his father. Hurt with a pain so deep, she turned, pretending to look out of the window, but tears blotted her view. She prayed no-one would notice her trembling.

He might be killed! She might never see him again! Catherine clasped her hands together tightly. She heard her father say to Bernard, "I hope you will stay and rest for at least one night?"

When Bernard agreed, the earl said jovially, "Then we shall have a celebration meal tonight, and I shall ask you all to be my guests."

Excited that they had all been made welcome, no-one noticed the forced smile on Catherine's face.

She would not have Bernard's evening ruined by her looking overset like a silly pea goose! She told herself this as she took pains over her toilette later — wearing her favourite gown of apricot silk — that she would appear as bright and fun-loving as she hoped Bernard would always remember her.

★ ★ ★

The evening meal of leg of mutton, boiled with capers, roasted chicken with vegetable side dishes, followed by currant pie and jellies, was lit by a host of candles, and was a merry occasion.

After, they had retired to the drawing-room and the tea tray was brought in, Hubert delighted everyone by playing some popular tunes for them. But as the evening progressed, Catherine was convinced Bernard was deliberately avoiding her.

Disappointed he did not seem to want to spend his last few hours in her company, she went to her bedchamber, saying little to her maid who hung up her clothes, and left her when she lay down to sleep. She felt too drained to cry.

She was quite unaware of Bernard slipping into her bedchamber, so quietly she did not hear or see him until she was aware of him sitting gently on the edge of her bed.

"I thought it best to slip off early tomorrow morning and not say goodbye, but I had to see you," he said in a hushed voice.

It may have seemed outrageous to others, him being here in her bedchamber — and yet it wasn't for them. They had shared privations and dangers in the past few weeks with a closeness that made this present situation seem perfectly normal to Catherine.

"I would have been most put out if you had done that!" she said quietly, yet trying to lift the tone of her voice to prevent him from feeling she might weep.

She watched his familiar features lit by the candle he carried, his dark eyes and knit brows looking intently at her. What could she say to this man she knew might be going to his death? She felt no fear, only a desire to say what was in her heart.

"Bernard, I know you are right to go to Paris — to assist your father. My love goes with you, you know that, don't you?"

For some seconds he looked at her, longing to clasp her in his arms to obliterate the agony in his mind. But she was showing admirable restraint, and so must he.

"Farewell, Catherine," he said, his words and eyes smooth and full of worship. "I will return as soon as I am able to," and so saying, he rose and left her, not daring to do as much as give her a chaste kiss.

10

"WHO is that charming girl over there, Madame Barbier? She really is most beautiful, and so graceful."

Mrs Harriet Hardy spoke excitedly, pointed her fan in the direction of the double doors to the white and gilt saloon of Lance Court. Mrs Hardy, a doyenne of Somerset society, seated as upright as the wall behind her, liked to know all the local girls searching for husbands. A coming-out ball was her chance to assess all such young ladies.

Madame Barbier looked across at the bevy of chattering, fashionable young ladies who had just made their entrance into the salon.

"Which one, Harriet? There are so many attractive girls here tonight," she said, smilingly.

"The young lady I'm talking about is the dark girl in the elegant taffeta silk with the blue bows down the front."

"Why, Harriet, you should recognise the host's daughter, none other than the beautiful Lady Catherine!"

Mrs Hardy hid a gasp.

"You don't mean to tell me that beautiful girl is Lady Catherine? It can't be!"

"Mrs Hardy, I should know," Madame Barbier said dryly.

Mrs Hardy's matronly head started, shaking the two tall ostrich feathers in her head-dress.

"Well, you surprise me, Madame Barbier. I always thought Lady Catherine, was ... at least people said she was, a hoyden!"

Madame Barbier acted like a ruffled hen.

"Really, Harriet, how can you think such a thing! Why Catherine is most genteel — just look at her."

Mrs Hardy fanned herself for some minutes. She was never ill-informed about any social scandal in her district.

"But, I remember years ago Catherine was so high-spirited she was expelled from school. Her father despaired of her!"

Madame Barbier retorted, "Well, he doesn't now! Why do you think he is giving this coming-out ball for her?"

Not to be out-done, Mrs Hardy whispered behind her fan, "What about the gossip?"

"What gossip?"

Mrs Hardy preened herself as Madame Barbier's bulging eyes stared at her.

"There is talk, much talk about Lady Catherine. She is said to have had some terrible experiences getting out of France recently. I hear she's infatuated with an impoverished, French nobleman, and that she came home with a whole boatload of French emigrés."

Mrs Hardy paused, hoping she had impressed upon Madame Barbier that Lady Catherine's conduct was not considered to be faultless.

Indignantly, Madame Barbier snorted.

"I came out of France with Catherine. There was nothing improper — "

"No?"

"No. And as to the Marquis de Clichy's son, why, if you met him, you would know he is a most honourable gentleman. He is, after all, a distant relative of mine."

Realising she had gone a little too far, Mrs Hardy tried to pacify Madame Barbier by saying that, of course, the nobility was not under the same constraints as the rest of society. They had a high-born right to do as they liked.

Madame Barbier snorted again, and Mrs Hardy was glad to hear the diversion of some lively dance music starting up, drawing their attention towards the younger guests who were beginning to fidget as if their feet were trying to answer the call of the lively music.

Catherine, whose charm had captivated every guest's attention, knew she was expected to lead the first dance of her coming-out ball. And she did not care much which young man she danced with.

Just as she had not given her full attention to the shopping expeditions in Bath; the hours spent visiting the mantua-maker and hairdresser, in preparation for the many concerts, routs and social calls she would be expected to attend.

She was living part of her life in a dream, unable to concentrate fully on anything — except anxiously wondering about Bernard's fate. It was already springtime, and since he'd left, over the long winter months, they'd heard nothing.

The chinless, young man who pushed himself forward to request to dance with her was a childhood friend of her brothers. Orlando Effingham was a good dancer, and Catherine was happy enough to accept him as her dance partner.

It was a warm, August evening, and as the dancers filled the floor, the saloon became unbearably hot and stuffy. She heard Orlando say, "Shall we slip away for a stroll in the cool of the garden?"

She should have noticed the desire in his eyes and refused to wander out into the night unaccompanied by her chaperone. But her independence during her flight from France had made her careless of such social strictures.

Amusing her with his small talk as he promenaded arm-in-arm along a shrubbery path, Catherine suddenly came to her senses.

"I think we should return to the saloon now, Orlando."

"Fa-la-la-la, Lady Catherine." He flounced his perfumed handkerchief, as he spoke. "How about a kiss first?"

Catherine's mind cleared as her body stiffened.

"I think not, Orlando."

"Why not? Your brothers tell me you are no goody-goody and are game for anything!"

Panic stirred in Catherine's breast

making her pulse beat fast.

"Not so, Orlando," she rejoined, trying to snatch her hand from his arm.

As he held her fast she cried, "Sir, I beg of you, leave go of me! You know I must return to my guests."

He still made no movement to let her go so in a moment of sheer anger she promptly slapped his face.

Shrinking away from him, Catherine felt she could not face returning to the ball. All she could think of was to hide herself away from these cruel tongue-wagging socialites. The dictators of society had no mercy for those to whom misfortune fell.

Orlando's mocking laughter followed her as she picked up her skirts to run. Suddenly a tall shadow loomed across her path. She screamed as firm hands held her.

Her struggling stopped as she recognised who it was . . . the strength in the arms which encircled her protectively. It was Bernard holding her!

"You impudent puppy dog!" Bernard's voice boomed, silencing Orlando's cackle. "Were you anything like a man, I might challenge you to a duel. I suggest you apologise to the lady this instant, sir, or feel the toe of my boot!"

Catherine was shivering and felt she had lost the strength to stand, and may have fallen were it not for Bernard's support. Heartfelt relief to see him alive was tempered with the humiliation of being found in such a compromising position.

Tears of relief and despair flooded her eyes so that she did not hear Orlando's apology, nor see him slink away. Neither was she aware of the tears in Bernard's eyes. His blood was afire; dangers and sorrows behind him, he had expected nothing but joy on his return. Composure took time.

"It's no use, Bernard," she murmured snuggling close to him.

"What's no use, Catherine?" he said fearfully. He'd prayed there would be no impediment now to their love.

Her tear-stained face looked up at his noble features.

"I have been condemned by society for being indecorous. The likes of Orlando have such a low opinion of me."

"Indeed. And why have you been deemed so? Have you been up to no good in my absence?"

"No. Just sailing down the Loire with you is considered to be too . . . too intimate."

Bernard hugged her closer, whispering in her delicate ear.

"Ignore them. It doesn't matter what they think. I think it was a very precious time in our lives. Do you remember the swing I made for your birthday?"

Catherine's eyes sparkled, watching his lips twitch as he offered her his clean handkerchief.

"Oh, yes! I'll never forget — it was an adventure." She took a deep breath to recover from her bout of sobbing.

"And dancing by the river with you, to the magical sound of Hubert's violin . . . I never wanted it to end."

"Nor I."

Their lips met for a long kiss that removed everything but pleasure from Catherine's mind.

She surfaced at last to say, "My guests will think me rag-mannered to have left them for so long."

"All you have to say is that you have been gone awhile because you have been accepting the hand of the Marquis de Clichy in marriage."

"The Marquis?" Catherine froze.

Bernard nodded, his face now solemn.

"I regret to say my father did not survive long in prison. His heart was weak. I understand he was given the comfort of a priest, and clean conditions in which to die in peace."

For a few moments they stood in silence, remembering a man they had both loved. Bernard cleared his throat.

"My father left me a considerable fortune in the English bank, Coutts.

So we can start to look for a fine country house, Catherine."

"And you can buy some horses."

"Indeed I will — although the memory of my beloved Golden Star will always live on in my heart," he said picking up and kissing a lock of her ebony hair.

They looked at each other and kissed again with hearts bursting like the buds of spring around them, ready to start their new life.

Both looked so radiantly happy as they entered the ballroom together. No-one wanted to express any indecorum shown by Catherine's absence, nor could they fault her handsome companion. The two were so obviously deeply in love.

THE END

WITH SOMEBODY ELSE
Theresa Charles

Rosamond sets off for Cornwall with Hugo to meet his family, blissfully unaware of the shocks in store for her.

A SUMMER FOR STRANGERS
Claire Hamilton

Because she had lost her job, her flat and she had no money, Tabitha agreed to pose as Adam's future wife although she believed the scheme to be deceitful and cruel.

VILLA OF SINGING WATER
Angela Petron

The disquieting incidents that occurred at the Vatican and the Colosseum did not trouble Jan at first, but then they became increasingly unpleasant and alarming.

DOCTOR NAPIER'S NURSE
Pauline Ash

When cousins Midge and Derry are entered as probationer nurses on the same day but at different hospitals they agree to exchange identities.

A GIRL LIKE JULIE
Louise Ellis

Caroline absolutely adored Hugh Barrington, but then Julie Crane came into their lives. Julie was the kind of girl who attracts men without even trying.

COUNTRY DOCTOR
Paula Lindsay

When Evan Richmond bought a practice in a remote country village he did not realise that a casual encounter would lead to the loss of his heart.

ENCORE
Helga Moray

Craig and Janet realise that their true happiness lies with each other, but it is only under traumatic circumstances that they can be reunited.

NICOLETTE
Ivy Preston

When Grant Alston came back into her life, Nicolette was faced with a dilemma. Should she follow the path of duty or the path of love?

THE GOLDEN PUMA
Margaret Way

Catherine's time was spent looking after her father's Queensland farm. But what life was there without David, who wasn't interested in her?

HOSPITAL BY THE LAKE
Anne Durham

Nurse Marguerite Ingleby was always ready to become personally involved with her patients, to the despair of Brian Field, the Senior Surgical Registrar, who loved her.

VALLEY OF CONFLICT
David Farrell

Isolated in a hostel in the French Alps, Ann Russell sees her fiancé being seduced by a young girl. Then comes the avalanche that imperils their lives.

NURSE'S CHOICE
Peggy Gaddis

A proposal of marriage from the incredibly handsome and wealthy Reagan was enough to upset any girl — and Brooke Martin was no exception.

A DANGEROUS MAN
Anne Goring

Photographer Polly Burton was on safari in Mombasa when she met enigmatic Leon Hammond. But unpredictability was the name of the game where Leon was concerned.

PRECIOUS INHERITANCE
Joan Moules

Karen's new life working for an authoress took her from Sussex to a foreign airstrip and a kidnapping; to a real life adventure as gripping as any in the books she typed.

VISION OF LOVE
Grace Richmond

When Kathy takes over the rundown country kennels she finds Alec Stinton, a local vet, very helpful. But their friendship arouses bitter jealousy and a tragedy seems inevitable.

CRUSADING NURSE
Jane Converse

It was handsome Dr. Corbett who opened Nurse Susan Leighton's eyes and who set her off on a lonely crusade against some powerful enemies and a shattering struggle against the man she loved.

WILD ENCHANTMENT
Christina Green

Rowan's agreeable new boss had a dream of creating a famous perfume using her precious Silverstar, but Rowan's plans were very different.

DESERT ROMANCE
Irene Ord

Sally agrees to take her sister Pam's place as La Chartreuse the dancer, but she finds out there is more to it than dyeing her hair red and looking like her sister.

HEART OF ICE
Marie Sidney

How was January to know that not only would the warmth of the Swiss people thaw out her frozen heart, but that she too would play her part in helping someone to live again?

LUCKY IN LOVE
Margaret Wood

Companion-secretary to wealthy gambler Laura Duxford, who lived in Monaco, seemed to Melanie a fabulous job. Especially as Melanie had already lost her heart to Laura's son, Julian.

NURSE TO PRINCESS JASMINE
Lilian Woodward

Nick's surgeon brother, Tom, performs an operation on an Arabian princess, and she invites Tom, Nick and his fiancé to Omander, where a web of deceit and intrigue closes about them.

THE WAYWARD HEART
Eileen Barry

Disaster-prone Katherine's nickname was "Kate Calamity", but her boss went too far with an outrageous proposal, which because of her latest disaster, she could not refuse.

FOUR WEEKS IN WINTER
Jane Donnelly

Tessa wasn't looking forward to meeting Paul Mellor again — she had made a fool of herself over him once before. But was Orme Jared's solution to her problem likely to be the right one?

SURGERY BY THE SEA
Sheila Douglas

Medical student Meg hadn't really wanted to go and work with a G.P. on the Welsh coast although the job had its compensations. But Owen Roberts was certainly not one of them!

HEAVEN IS HIGH
Anne Hampson

The new heir to the Manor of Marbeck had been found. But it was rather unfortunate that when he arrived unexpectedly he found an uninvited guest, complete with stetson and high boots.

LOVE WILL COME
Sarah Devon

June Baker's boss was not really her idea of her ideal man, but when she went from third typist to boss's secretary overnight she began to change her mind.

ESCAPE TO ROMANCE
Kay Winchester

Oliver and Jean first met on Swale Island. They were both trying to begin their lives afresh, but neither had bargained for complications from the past.

CASTLE IN THE SUN
Cora Mayne

Emma's invalid sister, Kym, needed a warm climate, and Emma jumped at the chance of a job on a Mediterranean island. But Emma soon finds that intrigues and hazards lurk on the sunlit isle.

BEWARE OF LOVE
Kay Winchester

Carol Brampton resumes her nursing career when her family is killed in a car accident. With Dr. Patrick Farrell she begins to pick up the pieces of her life, but is bitterly hurt when insinuations are made about her to Patrick.

DARLING REBEL
Sarah Devon

When Jason Farradale's secretary met with an accident, her glamorous stand-in was quite unable to deal with one problem in particular.

THE PRICE OF PARADISE
Jane Arbor

It was a shock to Fern to meet her estranged husband on an island in the middle of the Indian Ocean, but to discover that her father had engineered it puzzled Fern. What did he hope to achieve?

DOCTOR IN PLASTER
Lisa Cooper

When Dr. Scott Sutcliffe is injured, Nurse Caroline Hurst has to cope with a very demanding private case. But when she realises her exasperating patient has stolen her heart, how can Caroline possibly stay?

A TOUCH OF HONEY
Lucy Gillen

Before she took the job as secretary to author Robert Dean, Cadie had heard how charming he was, but that wasn't her first impression at all.

ROMANTIC LEGACY
Cora Mayne

As kennelmaid to the Armstrongs, Ann Brown, had no idea that she would become the central figure in a web of mystery and intrigue.

THE RELENTLESS TIDE
Jill Murray

Steve Palmer shared Nurse Marie Blane's love of the sea and small boats. Marie's other passion was her step-brother. But when danger threatened who should she turn to — her step-brother or the man who stirred emotions in her heart?

ROMANCE IN NORWAY
Cora Mayne

Nancy Crawford hopes that her visit to Norway will help her to start life again. She certainly finds many surprises there, including unexpected happiness.

UNLOCK MY HEART
Honor Vincent

When Ruth Linton, a young widow with three children, inherits a house in the country, it seems to be the answer to her dreams. But Ruth's problems were only just beginning . . .

SWEET PROMISE
Janet Dailey

Erica had met Rafael in Mexico, where their relationship had been brief but dramatic. Now, over a year later in Texas, she had met him again — and he had the power to wreck her life.

SAFARI ENCOUNTER
Rosemary Carter

Jenny had to accept that she couldn't run her father's game park alone; so she let forceful Joshua Adams virtually take over. But Joshua took over her heart as well!